A PAIR
for the
QUEEN

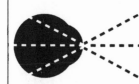

This Large Print Book carries the
Seal of Approval of N.A.V.H.

A Pair
for the
Queen

B. Comfort

Thorndike Press • Thorndike, Maine

Published in 1999 by arrangement with
W. W. Norton & Company, Inc.

Thorndike Large Print ® Senior Lifestyles Series.

The tree indicium is a trademark of Thorndike Press.

The text of this Large Print edition is unabridged.
Other aspects of the book may vary from the original edition.

Set in 16 pt. Plantin by Juanita Macdonald.

Printed in the United States on permanent paper.

Library of Congress Cataloging-in-Publication Data

Comfort, Barbara.
    A pair for the queen / B. Comfort.
      p. cm.
    ISBN 0-7862-2297-2 (lg. print : hc : alk. paper)
  1. McWhinny, Tish (Fictitious character) — Fiction.
2. Women detectives — Vermont — Fiction. 3. Vermont —
Fiction 4. Large type books. I. Title.
PS3553.O4832 P35   1999
  813'.54—dc21   99-050319

For Edna Jones,
who has enlivened many dog shows
and been generous with
her wit and wisdom.

One

Had I heard correctly? I was dismayed. Could my dear friend Hilary have made such a request? Hilary Oats, towering octogenarian soul of honor, archenemy of sleaze, tireless vilifier of the unmannerly, one who saves his greatest scorn for pretense . . . Could he have asked such a favor of me?

I wished I still smoked. It would have been the moment to go through the pleasant ceremony of lighting a cigarette, a time to formulate a clever biting response.

Sinking into my wing chair, I made room beside me for my pug, Lulu. "I have to assume, Hil, that this is some kind of a poor joke. Are you seriously asking me to produce a painting of some damn dog and sign it with someone else's name? Landseer? Or how about Rosa Bonheur? Or," I said sarcastically, "have you chosen some other particular artist for this highminded endeavor?"

Sarcasm isn't becoming to any of us, but it

was Hilary's turn. "Excuse me, Letitia, for offending your finer sensibilities."

I snorted, which was probably more acceptable than anything I might say, and got up and walked to the front door. "Bye-bye. I'm going to the dentist."

I headed for my car and climbed in, about to turn the key in the ignition.

"Tish, wait a minute, please. Let me explain. It's not as bad as I know it sounds. Would I ask you to do anything illegal?"

I tried to combine raising my eyebrows with a skeptical sneer.

"It's really just a fake forgery."

That stopped me. "A fake forgery — a bizarre redundancy from you, my dear. And utterly ridiculous. Unthinkable. And — what's the universal question? — why me?"

"Tish." Hilary picked up Lulu and put her beside me in my old Isuzu Trooper. "Tish, wait a minute. It's for Bruce."

Bruce — hapless Bruce Hemphill, Hilary's beloved godson. I remembered years before hearing Alice and Hilary talk about Bruce's visits to Lofton. Tales of his antics. His mishaps. Leg splints, arm slings, and eye patches. But mainly I heard Hilary's indulgent, adoring voice praising the jolly little tyke. The only time I met Bruce — or maybe I didn't actually meet him — was one serene July twilight when he found his way into the church belfry and roused the town with the kind of wild clanging normally reserved for dire emergencies. This from a bell more accustomed to being heard for a melodious half minute on Sunday mornings.

Bruce. My Lord, he must be forty or forty-five. I tried to think what reports had drifted my way about his doings in the last decade or so.

Years back I seemed to remember Hilary going to his wedding. Or was it a child's christening somewhere in the midwest? Then I recalled the time when Bruce, touring Africa, had returned with three thousand uniforms he'd bought from the Zulus that he hoped to sell to the Banana Republic, which was not receptive to the idea. Another lofty foray of his into the business world involved Captain Queeg-type marbles designed to be fingered by harried executives. Then, just lately, I had heard Hilary telling my niece Sophie that Bruce was somehow involved in dog shows.

Dogs. Ah, that had to be the connection. Now I could relax and drop any pretense of indignation. Happy, bumbling Bruce was drawing loving Hilary into another of his ill-fated schemes, but at least it sounded amusing. I mean, what could be complicated or risky about dog shows?

I had to smile. "So Bruce is behind this nutty idea. What in the world does he want with a dog portrait — a forgery?"

"Maybe I haven't told you, Tish, but Bruce's been trying to find himself, to find his niche for the last year or so since his divorce; and because he really is a good salesman, I'm happy to report he's starting his own business as a concessionaire at dog shows."

"A what? You mean he'll be selling hot dogs and ice cream?"

"No, no. They sell all kinds of things at shows now. When did you last go to a dog show?"

"Mmmm. I think I was eight years old, maybe ten; and I want you to know that Peppy won a blue ribbon, too, for the dog with the curliest coat."

"Well, in case you want to write this down — you ready? — things have changed. Bruce is going to sell dog art." Hilary held up a big hand. "Don't ask me what that means, Tish, but he wants a painting that looks like a billion dollars — something Christie's would sell. He wants to attract would-be collectors and the canine crowd in general. He wants to be noticed."

"And," I added, "he wants to see me in jail."

"Reserve judgment, Tish. He'll be up here next week. He wants to show me his new mobile store."

"Let me guess" — I started the engine — "a mobile store in which you just may have a tiny financial interest?"

Hilary shrugged and smiled happily. "It'll be fun to see him — and, Tish, prepare yourself: he'll be here for the First Day dance."

Our town had jumped the gun in many ways. A food coop, great waste disposal, and shared street-cleaning chores; but one of its livelier concepts was getting a head start on Independence Day festivities. I don't remember when it started, but Hilary tells me the idea was to have fun and get a little smashed at a dance on July third and walk it off the next day while waving flags and hoisting toddlers. However, that bacchanalian concept had been frowned on recently by the conservative young set, so we changed the date of the annual dance to fall on the first day of summer.

As I headed down the road, I thought about Hilary's request. I decided that the dog-painting scheme was just one of Bruce's harebrained ideas, so I felt sure his feelings wouldn't be hurt if I sat this one out.

Maybe not every dog show would welcome Bruce's accident-prone presence, but as Hilary had often said, Bruce was great fun and added a lot to any occasion.

As the only patient in Dr. Ernest Crater's waiting room, I relaxed in the good doctor's Boston rocker and felt my customary gratitude for his thoughtfulness.

When I heard myself humming "Old Rockin' Chair's Got Me," I popped to my feet. Oh, no, not yet it hasn't got me, I told myself. I touched my toes and then pulled up into a high stretch and caught sight of myself in a tall, skinny mirror over the magazine rack.

Good Lord, was I really seventy-seven? Yup, I could tell by my gray hair and my unlifted face. It has been said, ad nauseam, that one grows to look like one's dog. However, I think that's a canard, a lot of nonsense. I had a poodle for fifteen years, and I am neither long nosed nor fluffy. However, I must admit my resemblance to Lulu has been noted by some — though I'm not quite as warm eyed and friendly as my little friend, and I don't wiggle my tail all that much.

My would-be niece, Sophie, says I look like an old preppie. I think it's my late husband, Doug's, button-down shirts and my lifetime supply of turtlenecks. When Hilary is trying to butter me up, he uses more flattering terms. My detractors, I've heard tell, describe me as snooty and aloof, which is just plain silly.

I pulled out a hankie and wiped off my lipstick. Or, I should say, my makeup, because my idea of makeup is lipstick and maybe a dab of powder — though for dressy occasions, I do stick my finger in a couple of jars of this and that and add a little eye shadow and mascara.

I only recognize myself face front. I have trouble with a second mirror. Matter of fact, the only mirror in which I really look great is my car's rearview mirror; I've considered installing one in the bathroom. Now, thanks to looming cataracts, I had to put my nose almost on the waiting room mirror to check on the reason for my visit to the dentist: a chipped front tooth.

Shoving back my shoulders, I admired my yogic posture — all five feet two inches of it. I pulled in my chin, tucked in my fanny, and remembered what a little yogi had told me about walking properly. Imagine yourself being reeled in by a line attached to your pelvis. Try it.

I was trying it, gliding around the floor,

when I saw Dr. Crater's sadistic assistant standing in the doorway, rubbing her hands like an impatient executioner.

"Right this way, Mrs. McWhinny," she said and led me to my fate. Once in the chair, I was strangled by the bib chain and rendered helpless in an upside-down position. Ernie jammed all kinds of foreign matter in my mouth, including his assistant's left hand.

Sophie thinks our pudgy, ham-handed dentist should be called Dr. Info. There is nothing about Londonderry that he doesn't know, so he's become Ernie Info to us. Unlike many others of his unfortunate but necessary calling, Ernie Info didn't ask questions, thank goodness, but he talked all the time. He and Miss Arsenic reviewed last night's TV talk shows, and then they had a heated discussion about some damn TV show — all just millimeters above my face. I pointed at my chipped tooth and, unable to snort, gargled and bared my teeth like a hungry sled dog.

I've heard that dentists find their work so boring, they have to think of something else while they're working — but a sitcom? Damn it. My eyes were closed as I poked some part of the good doctor's anatomy with my elbow.

Back on track, Ernie took an impression of my tooth; and while the wax was hardening, he held it in place with his huge thumb. While involved in this life-threatening procedure, Ernie hit upon a topic of interest to me.

The land behind the Green Mountain shopping center had been chosen as the site for Londonderry's first dog show. It was to be billed as the first annual show, an event they hoped would bring people to Londonderry year after year.

My first selfish thought was: Oh, dear, why Londonderry? But of course I knew. Vermont was having hard times. I hated to contemplate an occasion that, while thrilling the Chamber of Commerce, would make our small mall unbearable. I could visualize our very own malfunction junction, what with the confluence of three roads plus the entrance and exit of our shopping center that all meet in a space that would be cramped for a game of hopscotch. What mayhem!

Another part of me looked forward to a dog show. Dogs had always played an important role in my life. When I was young I thought a family consisted of a mother, a father, children, a dog, and a cat. Years later when I fell in love with Doug, it was really his dog I fell for first.

I've never heard of any time or era when dogs were as cosseted as they are today. My friend Debbie, who owns a pet shop cum canine beauty parlor, once told me that within a radius of thirty-five miles there are thirty veterinarians, six other groomers, and at least twenty more enterprises that deal with the necessities as well as the frills of dogdom. Our supermarket has five shelves, each eighteen feet long, containing well over a dozen brands of dog food, including varieties for the young, the fat, the thin, and the elderly. You can find even more pet food next door in the hardware store.

From a contented dog's point of view, the show site is probably ideal. The field lies between the shopping center and the West River. There is always great and ample garbage available out behind the restaurant. A stationery store displays rack after rack of canine greeting cards for owners and handlers, and the drugstore beyond sells vitamins for pets.

Had I been a couple of decades younger, I'd probably have been working my tail off trying to make the show a success. Now I preferred the role of visitor and spectator. If Hilary had his way, however, I might just be an unwilling part of the show. But think positively, I told myself. It will be great fun.

16

Two

Driving up the Clement Hollow Road, I stopped the car when Sophie's farm, Goat Heaven, came into view. The tidy barn with its cupola sits in the middle of a fenced-in pasture on one side of the dirt road (which undoubtedly had once been just a cow path); on the other side, on a slight rocky rise, is Sophie's new house, open to the world like a giant bird cage waiting for a tenant.

The initial construction of a house — the bare posts and beams, the open spaces for windows and doors, and skeletal stairways — is usually much more interesting than the finished product. The armature, after being enclosed with plywood, wrapped in plastic, and covered with brick, clapboards, or, heaven help us, aluminum siding, often descends into mediocrity — or worse, fails to even register in one's eyes.

I felt sure that was not going to be the case with Sophie's dream house.

My cousin Marion in Hawaii married a

widower some time ago and inherited his two delightful children, Sophie and Sandy Beaumont. Sandy went back to the islands, having spent last fall in Lofton, but Sophie fell in love with New England.

After a few years at Dartmouth and a year gadding around France and Italy, which included an affair with an ersatz count, she became a photographer for a New York advertising agency. An assignment brought her to Weston, where we met a couple of years ago. We've been through a lot together. The happy highs outnumber the scary times, and it gives me great pleasure to claim her as my niece, while she in turn describes me as her aunt.

This past fall her crumbling old house had been dynamited into oblivion. With the help of our postmaster's son's backhoe and a cadre of his friends, Sophie had managed, before snowfly, to build a solid basement where her old house had been. And with a few professional house builders this spring, the new house had been framed out. With money from the insurance company and help from her father, Sophie had paid the builders to install an unfinished but usable bathroom and a kitchen with the bare essentials. Except for the roof and chimney, she was determined to build the rest of the house herself.

Carpentry soothes me. I love the smell of lumber. I enjoy the total absorption when I measure a board. I like a pencil between my teeth and a hammer dangling at my side. I like being able to admire what I've done and — not least — for some mysterious reason, I emerge from such a session with other unrelated problems solved.

It's my feeling that most artists are good carpenters. In my field, which is painting portraits for money — and painting, drawing, or creating whatever else occurs to me — there's always a lot of carpentry, cutting, sawing, and gluing. Then there's making frames and building crates, not to mention hefty work like fabricating and transporting folding screens or building a platform to paint a mural.

Hilary is all thumbs, but he loves surprising Sophie with offbeat gifts (he gave her the cupola for the barn last year). He was her senior adviser on the kitchen as well as her self-appointed account supervisor — a job she was glad to relinquish.

Sophie relies on me for elbow grease. I can no longer spend twenty minutes on my knees and reach around a two-by-four to screw on a brace or hammer a nail a foot away. I'd be stuck in a pose she'd never be able to undo. I prefer to work in dark corners, inventing shelves and little cupboards.

As I sat taking in her homestead, I saw Sophie farther down the road, talking to someone in a car. She waved at me and blew a kiss and returned to her conversation. I started up the Trooper and drove the quarter mile gap between us, then parked.

Walking toward the barn, I let myself into the corral to be greeted by a couple of goats I knew. Hairy Harry, a cadaverous old buck, presumed on our long friendship by taking a mouthful of my sweater. Ernie Info would have admired the way I pried open his teeth to reclaim my garment.

Except for a few of the regulars, Sophie's cashmere herd is in constant flux. Goat people seem to swap their animals or borrow or buy them. Does are whisked off for an assignation with someone's buck. Or Van Goat, Sophie's prize buck, is off calling on some neighborhood damsel.

"Hey, Tish." Sophie loped over to join me. It had been weeks since I had seen winsome, handsome Sophie wearing anything other than her present costume. Starting at the top, she wore a cotton country-store kerchief tied around her head Indian style, then a tattered T-shirt, and next a carpenter's apron bristling with nails hanging over her short Levi cutoffs. Her long legs ended in what appeared to be vintage paratrooper's boots.

I've resisted the temptation to paint Sophie. First, I know I could never get her to pose; and second, I know I couldn't do justice to her radiance. I admit to bias, and maybe that's what would be hard to catch in a painting. The contrast of her thick, dark eyebrows over gray-green eyes appeals to me. And no one wants a grinning portrait — at least I don't — but without Sophie's wide, hoydenish smile and what Hilary called her great set of choppers, it wouldn't be Sophie.

I have to content myself with just looking at her — or, more precisely, looking up at her.

"It'll be tonight, Tish — or tomorrow, for sure — we'll have kids." She straddled the top of the fence. "That's what I love." She hugged herself. "Kids, babies, little cashmere kids."

Hilary spent a lot of time worrying about Sophie. He thought she should be lavishing her maternal instincts on two-legged kids instead of four-legged ones. Not that he'd ever consider any potential father worthy of her.

"Agape" is the word for Hilary's feelings about Sophie, unconditional love. However,

21

her amorous antics drive him crazy. Not that he's antiamour, but the cast of suitors that have dogged Sophie are, in his opinion, beneath contempt. "Inept" is the mildest word I ever heard him use. He calls them brutes, pansies, opportunists, ignoramuses, and crooks.

Sophie reveres Hilary's opinion about her Hollandaise sauce but ignores his fulminations about her love life.

Hilary is right when he insists that she has never exhibited good judgment in men. Any cad or oily smoothie or buck with no pedigree can make her fall over like a nine pin. Sophie has what we used to call "round heels."

Thank goodness I don't worry about her love life. According to Hilary, no one can tell anyone else who to love or how to spend their money, so what's the use? I have faith in Sophie's ultimate good sense, even though her youth and animal vitality have landed her in quite a few pickles.

So what's new? Thinking about my own salad days makes me wince. Of course, that was way back before the sexual revolution, but it was also a time before AIDS, when you didn't have to compare blood tests before a little hanky-panky.

Anyway, I refuse to concern myself with

who's hanging whose hat where. I'll let Hil fret for both of us.

Sophie slid off the fence and plucked Lulu out of the window, kissing the top of her silky head. "Let's go check out the horses," she said.

Popeye spotted us first and neighed, revealing teeth that would give Ernie Info a heart attack. Sophie adopted the old gray horse last year when I bought my aged mare, Trixie. We figured my grizzled old dame was at least twenty, but she wanted no part of a quiet retirement. She banged my shoulder with her fuzzy chin while Lulu crooned a greeting.

We let the horses out to join the goats in the pasture while we sat on the mounting stone to admire the pastoral scene.

"It's beautiful, isn't it?" Sophie sighed with contentment.

"I'll say." I pointed. "Looks as though Tiffany's going to have twins."

"Could be, but I wasn't looking at her. I'm looking at the roof. I really think it's the greatest roof I've ever seen. The red ones are too red, and the green ones too green, and those silvery ones hurt your eyes. Don't you think mine's just perfect?" I nodded. "And you should hear it in the rain. It's heavenly. And just think — I'll never have a leak."

I gave her a congratulatory hug, and we sat in silence for a few minutes longer. Then I dumped Lulu off my lap and stretched. "I've got lots to do today, and I'd better get going. Who's that?"

A gray Mercedes was coming down the dirt road at a snail's pace. The car paused, and the occupants conspicuously examined Sophie's structure. When they came by the pasture, the male driver stared at us. The woman beside him, or maybe she was a child, looked at us, too.

"Creeps." Sophie sneered. "Talk about rubbernecking. What do we look like, an accident?" She opened the gate. "Did I tell you, Tish, about Kim? She's going to move in soon. She said she likes to sand things. I can use her."

"Kim?"

"Yeah, Kim. Oh, maybe you never met her. She was on the ski team at Bowdoin. I skied against her. We got to be friends. Saw her in Boston last winter. That was her I was just talking to in the car. Should have introduced you, but she was in a hurry. Says her family is around here someplace this summer."

Sophie has been living in her kitchen, which is the same shape as mine — longer than it is wide to accommodate a table at one end. That's where Sophie sleeps, on a cot, pushed against the studs. I didn't ask where she was going to put her friend. Sophie hates questions like that, and why should I care? I don't, unless someone considers either of my guest rooms available.

I love Sophie, I really love her, but she'd been living with me ever since her house exploded five long months ago. For a decade now, ever since Doug died, I've become accustomed to the luxury of living alone and increasingly resentful about sharing my space. Sophie seemed to be constantly parading through the house with and without friends and with little regard for conventional hours. I found it really quite irritating. It was her opposite behavior that was even worse. She'd have a spell of thoughtfulness and in an effort not to awaken me would turn knobs as quietly as a thief at night. Then she'd tiptoe upstairs and close doors making only the tiniest sound.

As much as Hilary adores Sophie, he hated the tiptoeing, too. Like me Hilary found having Sophie around to be a strain. He was full of anxiety that she might walk in on us expressing a rush of affection frequently brought on by one of Hil's epicurean dinners replete with wine from his precious cellar.

In the last year Hilary and I added a new dimension to our relationship: sex. Which is not to say we sit about salivating or race each other to the bedroom. A couple of half-baked affairs since my late husband, Doug, died had left me unenthusiastic about senior suitors, and without really thinking about it I imagined Hilary had accepted a sexless old age as inevitable after his wife died. We were both delighted to find that such was not the case. We accept our shortcomings, and fortunately we don't take ourselves too seriously.

My bed was designed for regular-sized people, and six foot four Hilary claims it's impossible to spend a whole night in such pain, which suits my peculiar ways. I like to get up in the morning and go about my life unburdened by social niceties or company for breakfast.

Because Hilary is always wandering in and out of my house, I don't suppose our neighbors are surprised to see him striding home in the moonlight or rolling home on stormy nights looking like a bell buoy in his yellow slicker. Not that he gives a hoot what anyone thinks. Except for Sophie.

I think the older you get, the less you care what other mortals think about you — a generality Hil would hate.

From Sophie's point of view, I guess that she regards the old as dead from the neck down and, short of joining us in bed, wouldn't believe that we were up to anything more than happily bundling and probably playing our usual game of Scrabble under the most comfortable conditions.

I must give Sophie credit. She had tried to find a room elsewhere and succeeded in renting a place for January. But it hadn't worked out because the landlord developed a crush on her, and his wife wisely suggested that Sophie find other quarters.

It wasn't just the landlord's unfortunate amorous condition that had brought her back to me. I had urged her to move back into the yellow guest room, which by now was known as Sophie's room. I hate to think of myself as selfish and heartless, and I knew that Sophie really had to be close to her beloved cashmere goats. My house in Lofton was as close as you could get to Clement Hollow — with the exception of Newton Cleary's farm. He's her neighbor, and while we knew he had plenty of extra room, Sophie had been apprehensive about attracting the not quite invisible halo of gnats, or whatever they were, that came in and out with the dear old fellow.

Newt begins and ends every remark or

greeting by pushing back his old felt hat and scratching his head. Reason enough, I'd thought (imagining Sophie's honey-colored hair infested with bugs), for her to move back to Lofton with me.

Oh, well, why talk about it. It was over now.

When the roofers had come to install Sophie's handsome black-metal roof, I was thrilled. Thrilled because that was the event that triggered her departure. Hilary had also been thrilled, and I don't need to tell you how thrilled Sophie was — not only to leave, but also to move into her very own house, or at least part of it.

I'm sure we all exhaled a long breath of relief that we'd managed our togetherness with nary a snarl or cross word.

I gave Sophie a final hug and opened the Isuzu's door. Lulu hopped in, and I followed. Lulu looked out at the heavenly Vermont landscape on what was almost the first day of spring. I leaned sideways in the car and tweaked her velvet ear. "Aren't we lucky?"

She responded to my familiar statement with a contented grunt.

Three

Our country store is the modest centerpiece of Lofton Village. It is yellow — not lemon yellow or stop-sign yellow, but a lovely custard yellow. The saltbox building has been painted so many times, it has acquired a patina that makes me think of early ceramics. Down the road you can just see the Lofton Inn, a cluster of white buildings snuggled under ancient maple trees. Next door to my house is our classic New England church and beyond it, Millie's library with its huge bay window offering an invitation to come in. We are so used to seeing Peter's garage, which is a small addition to his house that no one regards it as an eyesore on our picture-perfect Main Street. The post office is directly opposite my house, and at the other end of the street the Walkerses' handsome barn has been turned into an antiques shop.

Half a century ago little Loftonites could learn how to count by pointing at cows. Today they count tourists with cameras or out-of-state license plates.

There are five hundred voters in Lofton, hundreds of summer and fall residents, and skiers galore. Our population includes artists, writers, performers, and, more recently, bridge players and golfers. We have horse people and dog people and bird watchers. There is an increasing group of retirees with a zest for living, and there are young people like Sophie raising goats and sheep. Others sell their crafts and export homemade food. "Made in Vermont" has become a powerful sales pitch.

The store is run by a consortium, determined to keep its charm and sophisticated simplicity intact. Those of us on the committee all too frequently have the difficult job of finding people for the job of storekeeping — and once again we had to do so because our last storekeepers picked up and moved to Boston.

Our hope was to find an agreeable and capable couple who wanted to live in Vermont — in the apartment over the store that went with the job — were charmed by Lofton, and didn't mind hard work.

We've had some disasters and some winners. I made it clear to the committee that my current term would be my last. Because I live diagonally across the street, I'm perceived as the person in charge, which has become a big pain in the neck. Besides, with all of the young people moving into town, it was someone else's turn to share the applause and the blame.

Millie Santini, the committee secretary and super-wonderful town librarian, had done the initial vetting of the couple we planned to interview after lunch. All I knew was that Millie said the man sounded great on the phone, but she hadn't talked to Mrs. What's-her-name because she was at work. And what did she do? Millie had asked. Her husband said she was a model. ("Gimme a break," Sophie had said. "You're not hiring a model, are you? You know our road commissioner's a sex maniac. We'll never get him out of the store.") And after a little more questioning, Millie had gathered that the missus squirted perfume on customers in the cosmetics section of Bloomingdale's.

Now, sitting on my front porch, I tried to open my mouth Ernie Info style to eat the overloaded cucumber sandwich I often favored for lunch. I put it aside to watch the same Mercedes that Sophie and I had seen earlier come to a stop in front of the library.

Oh, Lord, a man who stared rudely at strangers and a woman who sprayed unwilling victims with Lord-knows-what. They had to be our candidates.

An hour later, I melted as Jeremy Blount enveloped my hand in his and in a delicious deep voice told me how glad he was to meet me. So much for prejudgments. In seconds I realized who he looked like. Find a nickel, a nice, new shiny one, and look at the bas-relief of Thomas Jefferson.

Blount was slim and fine boned, but sturdy. His very high forehead was accented by even eyebrows and an aquiline nose. He even sported a smaller version of Jefferson's ponytail.

Blount's Ivy League costume of gray slacks and a blue blazer became him. He reached behind and brought forth his minuscule mate. Or was she his daughter?

I had been under the impression that the emaciated, flat-chested gamine look was out of favor, but there she stood — all eighty-five pounds of her. She wore gauzy pasha pants and a white tank top that came down to her crotch. Long, complicated earrings just cleared her shoulders.

"This is my wife, Lily." Blount introduced her as I took her hand, and on closer inspection I saw that the tinkling earrings were made up of silver knives, forks, and spoons. I caught the alarm in Millie's eyes and knew we were thinking the same thing. The ear-rings conveyed a message: The poor young waif was starving.

Lily's short hair didn't seem to have the vitality to do anything but lie on her skull. It didn't even blow in the breeze. Her eyes were arresting and were taking me in like a professional phrenologist.

While sharing our gentle handshake, I wondered if she'd have the strength to pound the keys on our monster antique cash register.

Wispy Lily responded with concern, then delight, to a woof from the Mercedes and hurried over to open the door for a tan-and-black generic dog. I guessed its ancestry might include a Cairn or a beagle.

Blount smiled. "Where Lily goes, Whis-kers goes."

Whiskers dashed beyond us all to greet Lulu, whose tight little tail semafored her pleasure at the meeting.

They were joined by Lucifer, a huge St. Bernard who usually blocks the entrance to the store. I've watched tourists and natives alike heave and pull and push the great beast and try to cajole it to move — that is, until they spot the fly swatter hanging low beside the door above a sign: HIT HIS REAR END. Once hit, Lucifer will yawn, stretch, and rise. During the hot busy summer days, Lucifer sleeps in my flower bed. Thank goodness I'm a lousy gardener, so I don't mind a St. Bernard lying there among the impatiens. It's a lovely sight immortalized by many photographers.

There's always one busybody in every crowd, and in ours it's Charlie our postmaster's dog, Duke, who spends his days in front of the post office but thinks he owns the whole town. Spotting the newcomers, he trotted over and peed on the Mercedes' tires and then mushed around, rearranging the dog circle.

"Dogs, dogs, dogs." Millie pushed Duke and Lucifer away. "Come on, everyone. Let's go inside and do some talking."

The library is not officially open on Monday, so we adjourned to its bright inviting reading room. The whole place isn't much bigger than my living room, but Millie has turned it into heaven and a haven, too, for youngsters. They love to listen to Millie read and regard the library as a part of their lives. Millie's desk looked like a magic carpet. There must have been fifty books stacked in piles.

Millie's a peach, someone once said. Well, she is a peach and much more than that. Her frizzy white hair makes her look like a dandelion about to blow away. But no zephyr is about to waft her around. Her small feet are firmly planted on the ground, and we all know how lucky we are to have her eye on the small world of Lofton.

"This reference letter you sent me, Mr. Blount . . ."

"Jeremy."

"Jeremy," Millie said. "This company seems to have closed. My phone calls weren't answered."

"Oh, I know. I'm so sorry. They filed for Chapter Eleven just after Harvey wrote that letter. I should have mentioned that."

We talked for a long time. Jeremy Blount's distinguished look and engaging sincerity clearly captivated Millie.

Luther Marx, another member of our committee, asked Jeremy if he played golf. I'm sure every step of Luther's trip through life has been in pursuit of a golf ball. When Jeremy said yes, he did play golf, Luther beamed.

Luther gestured at us. "You girls decide."

"Girls? Good God, Luther," I said. "Haven't the females in your family ever straightened you out?"

"Yeah, yeah, yeah, it's all I hear." He glanced at his watch. "Hey, I gotta get home." He shook his hands over his head. "I vote yes."

Blount gave him an old-boy's handshake, assuring his admirer that he was the man for the job and that he had fallen in love with Lofton already.

"Young lady," Betsy Westervelt, our other member, spoke up. "About your costume — I'm sure it's very chic and very becoming, but I wonder if your work at Bloomingdale's has prepared you for our country image at the store."

Lily, quietly patting Whiskers, said something that sounded like "K mart." Betsy raised her hand. I always expect her to blow a whistle and we'd all play basketball. "Don't say a word, my dear. My skinny daughter, Kate, just your size, has left me a closet full of shirts, jeans, and sweaters. You'll be doing me a favor if you'll take them."

Lily smiled and rubbed her arms. "A sweater would be nice; it's cold up here. Thank you."

Jeremy put his arm around Lily in an avuncular fashion. "Before we settle anything, I do want to be sure we'll have the weekends off. You said that was OK. Right, Mrs. Santini?"

"That's fine. Hilda and Joe like to work on weekends."

We couldn't run the store without Hilda and Joe, gregarious retired city folk. They love playing store and put their earnings in a piggy bank for their grandchildren.

"Then it's settled. Thank you," Blount said. "It's so beautiful here." He embraced the village scene by spreading his arms, missing my head by millimeters. "I don't need to tell you that Lofton — in fact all of Vermont — is made for photographers, and I intend to make the best of it. If my pictures turn out to be salable, that will be a happy by-product. I'll be doing it for pleasure. I've promised to find a boat, maybe a canoe or double kayak, for my girl." He smiled for us. "We're going to be explorers."

And he meant girl. My Lord, she was barely a woman. But his use of the word made the disparity in their ages a little revolting. Blount had told Millie that he'd been in the ad business for years. I believed the "years" part. Guessing someone's age was not my strong point, but I felt sure he was ten years older than the forty he claimed. And Lily! I'd have to ask Sophie what she thought.

Betsy had obviously given the nod of approval to the Blounts by offering Lily her daughter Kate's clothes. Millie asked for my vote with her eyebrows. I nodded, put my hands in my pockets, and we all followed Millie's suit and stood up. "Okay," she said. "It's a deal, Mr. Blount."

"Jeremy, please," Blount said and shook our hands, while Lily murmured and Whiskers gave me her paw. "I'm a quick study," he said. "We'll be ready for business in no time."

With business settled, I walked back across the street and picked up where I had left off: sitting on my front porch, eating the remainder of my cucumber sandwich. I watched from my chair as Jeremy opened the trunk of his car and removed two suitcases, a backpack, and a briefcase.

There was no question about someone liking the cozy apartment upstairs over the store. I wondered if we would like them. Jeremy's questionable reference wasn't too good — but at least we always had a one-month trial agreement, and as long as the man wasn't a crook. . . .

I mean, what could go wrong? We have a few retired tycoons who like to flex their muscles and manage to spare time from focusing on a golf ball to oversee the store's books. It's not as though the proprietors unpack weekly shipments of Beluga caviar and truffles.

I wasn't going to worry. Today had been

my swan song so far as being store mother was concerned.

Having finished my sandwich, I was about to go inside when I noticed that the briefcase that Jeremy had taken out of his car was still outside, near the middle of the road. Because the expensive leather case was an inviting target for our Main Street dogs, I thought I'd better move it.

Sure enough . . .

"Oh, no, you don't!" I trotted across the road as Duke started to circle the briefcase and was about to lift his leg. When I reached for the case, the darn thing fell open and to my horror spilled its contents on the dusty dirt road. Cursing my fate, I knelt to gather up the manila envelopes, plastic viewing sheets for transparencies, and Lord knows what all.

"Good God, what are you doing?" Our new storekeeper's charm was missing as he rudely bumped me aside and grabbed the case out of my hands. Stuffing the rest of its contents back inside, the man literally fumed. "Did you open this? Did you look at my pictures?" He didn't wait for my denial and sputtered something that sounded like "old witch" — or more probably "old bitch." No "Thank you, Mrs. McWhinny, for retrieving my briefcase." No "Excuse me for knocking you over." I was thoroughly annoyed.

"Did I look at all of this stuff of yours, Mr. Blount? Of course," I said sourly. "I always go through briefcases I find in the middle of the road." I bared my teeth in a fake smile. "Now I know all your secrets."

With the case clutched to his chest, the angry man stomped into the store.

Well, the hell with him. I walked over to speak to Millie, who was crossing the street.

"I scared our storekeeper to death. Told him I inspected his briefcase — a briefcase so important he left it out in the middle of the road."

"What was in it?"

"Dunno — photographs or whatever. I bet he's a blackmailer. He probably has a picture of Hillary Clinton necking with Bob Dole."

After we tossed around a few more outlandish possibilities, I went on home.

Necessity overcame my disinclination to go over to the store because late in the day I was seized by an uncontrollable urge to polish my flat silver. I had spread it all out on the kitchen counter before discovering I had no silver polish.

As I approached the store, I could see Blount looking at me through the window. I hoped he was rehearsing the apology I felt was my due.

Inside the door I was briefly arrested by a towering stack of what must have been boxes of canned goods that were piled high on a tall skinny stool.

Then I saw something that made me smile. I was transported back to childhood when I spied a shiny fifty-cent piece on the floor. A vivid picture of my devilish little brother came to mind. The little monster used to plant such bait carefully wired to fool the next sucker, usually me. He'd be hiding behind the couch or a chair, waiting to yank the precious prize from a reaching hand. So instead of stooping as I might have, I walked on — and promptly had the daylights scared out of me as a few hundred pounds of cans crashed to the floor just behind me.

Lily dashed over and clutched my arm. "Oh, you might have been killed — I told you, Jeremy!"

"Shhh," a smiling Jeremy shushed his bride. "Quiet, quiet. You aren't hurt, are you, ma'am?" He was patting my other arm.

Too stunned to reply, I shrugged out of their hold. I wasn't hurt, but Lily's words rang in my ears: "You might have been killed."

It was an effort to be polite as Blount apologized. I watched him carrying the heavy cases out to the back storeroom. Was the man evil or incredibly stupid and careless? Banish the thought, I told myself. The man couldn't have arranged such a trap for me on purpose. I could hear Hilary's voice advising me not to look for trouble and Sophie's voice chiming in, too, saying, "Butt out, Tish, butt out."

Zombielike, I retrieved a jar of silver polish. Relax, I commanded myself. The new hired man doesn't know a can of beans from a cream puff. He'll learn. No way could he have intended to flatten me under that cascade of cartons.

Four

Back when my father was courting my mother, they were asked to leave the dance floor at the Copley Plaza in Boston for doing the turkey trot, and there I was almost eighty years later in Lofton doing Lord-knows-what like crazy. A couple we knocked into a ringside table said we were doing the monkey, or did they say donkey? Whatever I was doing, it wasn't what my partner was doing.

Under a gaslight on Copley Square, my father had tucked my mother into the front seat of his Stutz Bearcat and they drove away. It wasn't as simple for me. I'd said yes to Bruce when he asked me to dance, and I was damned if I'd quit before the band stopped playing.

Bruce was much as Hilary had described him, but better. While he was your basic amiable extrovert, he had a twinkle in his eye and an infectious smile. He was shorter than I had expected and quite hefty without being fat. I'm partial to bow ties; Bruce's number featured lightning stripes and hung askew, highlighting his jaunty demeanor. If I hadn't just had a demonstration of how quick and strong he was, I would have long since been flattened on the dance floor.

When we met, Bruce had seized my hands in both of his and almost kissed me, then seemed to think better of it upon realizing we were strangers. I daresay his natural puppy-dog friendliness put him in that group of people who think they should kiss any and all older women.

It would've been hard not to like Bruce's sweet face or to cast a cold eye on his effusive warmth. A lack of worldly success had obviously not dampened his spirits or his zest for life.

When the music stopped and I lurched back to our table, our postmaster, Charlie, reached out and grabbed my arm. "Way to go, Tish. When did you learn to do the hip-hop?"

I sank into my chair and kicked off my shoes. "Is that what I was doing?"

Bruce thought I had been doing the boogie. "Whatever it was, you really did it," he said, grinning.

He and I congratulated each other and gulped the beer that Hilary poured from a foaming pitcher. I considered pouring part of mine over my feet but remembered I'd offered to be part of the cleanup team in the morning.

Hilary excused himself to sit in with the band for the next set. The group consisted of Sam Elwood, who ran the sawmill and played a hot keyboard (what's happened to the old upright?); Janet, my hairdresser, who made beautiful music on saxophone; the new minister from Clement Hollow, who Sophie said played a sexy fiddle; and Millie's husband Joe, on drums.

In the city, the black case Hilary pulled out from under the table probably would have held a machine gun. Here at Lofton's First Day of Summer jamboree it held Hilary's ancient banjo. Everyone applauded its appearance.

The younger set was bemused that Hil could play so well — be so cool without having his banjo plugged into an electronic box.

The old-fashioned jazz the band began to play was designed to please Hilary. I liked it, too, and sat back to watch the dancers.

Bruce leaned over and put his plump hand over mine. "Will you do it, Tish?"

At first I thought he meant dance again; then I realized he was asking about the dog painting.

"Oh, Bruce, didn't Hilary tell you that I really can't consider it? I'm very busy gathering and cataloging some of my things, and I have a portrait to paint next week. I'm almost sure you can find someone on your dog show circuit who'll help you out."

"If you put it that way, of course I wouldn't want to interfere with your work." He sighed. "I'd never sell the painting, you know. I just need a great-looking painting that I can imply was done by some hot-shot old-timer. I just want to cause a stir." Bruce looked as though he might cry.

I was spared any further conversation about the unfortunate topic when Millie paused beside my chair. "Will you look at Sophie? Who's the guy she's with? An import?"

The wild virago dancing up a storm was indeed Sophie. The other dancers were giving her plenty of space. I should say "them." Her partner, whom I didn't recognize, was cavorting around like a madman. Even though I might possibly know him, anyone would've been unrecognizable under the circumstances.

"Who is he?" Hilary had rejoined us. He frowned. "Anyone we know?"

"Haven't the foggiest."

Bruce nudged me. But since he could see

my attention was drawn to the dance floor — or to be more precise, the grammar school basketball court — he asked Hilary, "Who's the gent with the ponytail?"

"He's the new fellow who is running our store. That pigtail looks silly on a grown man — but he's okay."

That Hilary liked Jeremy was a testimony to the man's charm. Possibly he excused the ponytail when on closer examination of a nickel he realized that the president's hairdo gave the fashion historical credibility. Jeremy had also endeared himself to Hilary when he said that while he, Jeremy, might not be the greatest proprietor for the store, he guaranteed that everyone would love Lily.

The Blounts looked sedate compared to the exuberant Loftonites: Jeremy formal and graceful, Lily demure and shy.

"She's like that model what's-her-name." Bruce remembered. "Twiggy."

Hilary massaged the point of his well-trimmed winter beard. "Seems to me he's got to be a father figure to that wisp of a girl. Makes you wonder, doesn't it, how a man his age snares such a young butterfly?"

"A moth," I said. "I think you mean a moth."

Hilary stuck out his lower lip. He doesn't

like being told what he means.

"I think she's just a moth mindlessly attracted to a strong light."

"Ah, well," Hilary said. "We mustn't judge anyone too quickly — and, better yet, not at all."

Hilary is extremely tolerant of the human race. He enjoys ugly ducklings as well as butterflies. He does require that the species that come his way have acceptable table manners, avoid generalizations, and shun double negatives. Clearly, Hil was attracted to Lily Blount. If the young lady was looking for Sir Walter Raleigh, Hilary was ready.

Sophie came wobbling off the dance floor. "Phew." She leaned over the back of my chair, poured a beer into my empty glass, and downed it like an old chug-a-lugger. "Hey, Tish, you still got that body cast from the time you fell out of a tree? I could use it."

A head-to-toe body cast of mine, if I had one, would barely reach Sophie's rib cage.

Hilary introduced Sophie to Bruce, then asked about her dancing partner. "Who is he?"

"Oh, him? That's George. He's a friend of a friend. You know, the friend I told you about, Tish. But what a performance *you* put on! Was that what they used to call jitterbugging?"

"No, dear. It was a Viennese waltz." Before we could discuss my position in the world of dance, a tall man tapped Sophie on the shoulder. I caught his Texas drawl and heard the blarney in his invitation to dance. Instantly they were lost among the gyrating revelers.

Hilary announced that he was leaving. "I've got to put my banjo to bed. Bruce, take care of Ginger Rogers, here, and see that she gets home. You two have fun."

Hilary was still making his way out of the gym when the tall Texan who had been dancing with Sophie bent over in a mock bow, pulled out the chair Hilary had vacated, and sat down.

"For Christ's sake, Bruce," he said. "What are you doing here? Don't tell me, I know. Dog shows, dog shows, dog shows."

He patted my arm. "Hello, sugar. I'm Jack." He turned back to Bruce. "So tell me where you're parking your rig."

Sugar, indeed. Who did the wooly-haired cowboy think he was? I put my glasses in my pocket and rose. "Good night, Bruce."

"Tish, wait a minute. I want you to meet Jack Conners. He's my . . ."

"Bruce is my trailblazer." Jack grinned and rubbed his big, knobby hands together. "Right, Bruce? Jean got tired of being married to Bruce, here, and decided to try me. Right, old man?"

I was surprised that Hilary hadn't said anything about Bruce's ex-wife being in Lofton, but maybe he didn't know they were.

Jack Connors was not a type to whom I was naturally attracted, and I definitely was not charmed by his takeover performance. But maybe I was just tired and Connors might look better in the light of day. I had a feeling that the man had moved himself into our lives.

I decided this was the perfect time to go home, and I stood up to leave. Brute force was required for me to hold Bruce down in his chair. "Don't get up. Please. I'm quite capable of getting home by myself."

Some friends heard me trying to persuade Bruce to let me leave, and I was swept up and out the door with them.

Before we said good night midway between my house and the store, everyone was talking about the Blounts. Lucy Wilson said she thought Jeremy was romantic — and very sexy. Tommy, her husband, said he thought Jeremy looked like a banker who wouldn't give you a loan. "Take it from me, he's a DP. Bet he's never been in the country before; looks like a city gigolo."

"Oh, Tommy, for heaven's sake," I said. "Give him a break or we'll elect you to find someone else." I admired my magnanimous spirit.

"Just kidding, Tish. Nothing wrong with the fella. Hey, I want to like them."

They both had more to say, but I had already opened my front door — without a key — and headed inside.

There was a growing consensus in the village, particularly on Main Street, that all the people who stopped to admire quaint Lofton were not innocent landscape lovers and cow watchers and that an open door was an invitation to trouble. But my feeling was that keys were for the city. I'd never locked my doors in Vermont, and in spite of what others said, I didn't plan to start now.

Lulu leaped off the sofa and practically walked up my front and into my arms. As I opened the door to let her out for her final walk of the day, I thought about my decision of the minute before to never lock my doors. If an intruder were to hurt Lulu or, heaven forbid, steal her, I think I'd die. When Lulu returned from her good-night visit to my neighbors' shrubbery, I watched her cobby little body vanish up the stairs and made a vow to change my casual ways.

I locked both the front and back doors.

Exhausted from all the dancing earlier, I filled my bathtub for a long hot soak.

The telephone rang as I emerged from the bathtub. It was Hilary, who said he'd been concerned that I'd be stuck with Bruce and would feel I had to entertain him. I told him I thought Bruce was a dear and that the Wilsons had walked me home, adding, "I met some big cowboy named Jack Connors, who said he's married to Bruce's ex-wife, Jean. What's the story?"

"No story, but I was not surprised to learn that they're here. Jean's a big deal in the dog world, or maybe was. I really don't know. Though Bruce says he's nice enough. But we'll talk tomorrow. Just wanted to make sure you got home safe and sound."

"Thanks, Hil. By the way, this Connors character is one of those big folksy jokers I can't stand, but I'm not surprised Bruce says he's nice. It's because your beloved godchild is nice. We really had a good time together."

"Please tell me that means you're going to help him out."

"Don't ask. Nightie night, sleep tight."

Talk about sleeping tight. I couldn't. Lying in bed, I was paying the penalty for mixing drinks. First a scotch before dinner, then wine with Hilary's sublime codfish cakes, and then that beer at the jamboree.

Unable to sleep, I did some thinking instead. Like Hilary, I was touched by Bruce and wondered if I was being a mean old witch. After all, if he wasn't going to sell the painting I suppose it wouldn't hurt me to help him. On the other hand, I couldn't see myself deliberately painting a picture that was supposed to be old or supposed to have been painted by someone else. What a job it would be trying to antique wooden stretchers — and aging the canvas would be almost impossible. No, I couldn't do it. That I could even think of doing such a thing embarrassed me.

Then I had an inspiration.

I thought of Alice Oats — Hilary's late wife who had died about when my husband, Doug, had, a decade ago. I adored Alice but could still remember vividly what hell it was to drive anyplace with the woman. No yard sale was too small or too tawdry to escape her eagle eye. She'd jam on the brakes at the sight of an old mower and other hodgepodge for sale, always certain that an undiscovered Monet or bit of Tiffany glass was hidden behind the barn door. She was known to every antiques dealer in New England and was on speaking terms with the custodians of the surrounding town dumps

— excuse me, I mean waste management areas.

I shouldn't complain because my generous friend often gave me great old frames that I could refinish or refurbish. Many of the props in my studio were gifts from Alice — the odd copper pot or a paintable chunk of fabric.

Much of her eclectic collection was stacked and piled in the loft of Hilary's barn. He had resisted all attempts and offers to dispose of Alice's treasures for worthy charitable causes. Hilary couldn't bear the thought of people who might not even have known Alice pawing over things that had meant so much to her. After she died, he said he didn't care what happened and made the cogent argument that anything of any value now would only be enhanced by time.

But what I was thinking about was a dog painting I remembered, or maybe two or three. Possibly one of them might be in reasonably good shape, and with a lick and a promise and a little varnish, I could patch it up to fill the bill for Bruce.

Delighted with my cerebrations, I looked at my watch. Dawn was a couple of hours away. I could hardly wait.

Five

The cleanup crew at the gym turned me down. Said they had more drudges than mops and brooms and didn't need my help.

Relieved, Lulu and I got our morning workout trotting along Main Street and up Hilary's driveway.

One expects Mama Bear, Papa Bear, and Baby Bear to emerge from Hilary's snug, brown-shingled bungalow. Inside, the place is a monument to ingenuity and happenstance. Part of the ceiling is propped up by a mast from Hilary's cutter, which died of old age on a Cape Cod shoal. Floor-to-ceiling bookshelves insulate two walls of the wandering living room. Paintings, photographs, charts, and indecipherable documents hang willy nilly without a horizontal line to share. His much admired coffee table in front of the ten-foot sofa is made entirely of coffee table books. The end tables are stacks of magazines and huge catalogs. Alice had no sense of order and, if possible, Hilary has even less; since she's been gone, the house looks totally askew. In spite of this, the place manages to have a wacky charm.

Hilary and Bruce were sitting on one side of the couch, and even though my eyesight isn't too great, I saw Hilary slip what I took to be his checkbook under *The New York Times.* I think he'd rather be thought of as a flint-eyed financier than the soft touch he is.

It would be easy and fun to indulge Bruce. I hoped he appreciated his godfather.

When I announced my nocturnal recall, Bruce jumped to his feet and clapped his hands. Bowing low, he kissed my hand, then grabbed Lulu and executed a little dance step.

"Right on, Letitia! Right on!"

Hilary sent us off to the barn with his blessing, giving us carte blanche in Alice's hayloft. He examined his wristwatch and told us we were expected back for breakfast promptly at nine.

A friend of mine once said, "Never send anyone who can read to fetch something from the attic." I knew what she meant.

There I stood, holding a fragile compote dish upside down, trying to read the marking on its bottom. In my other hand I clutched a mink-and-sequined cloak that might have been worn by my mother in the

Roaring Twenties. Bruce was babbling with joy about a set of golf clubs with wooden shafts; a tag on it said they had once belonged to President Woodrow Wilson. I put a hat aside when I spied a pack of stereopticon postcards of Italy before World War I.

I could almost see Alice's ghost grinning at our excitement and pleasure.

Bruce pointed to where screens, mirrors, and paintings were leaning against the wall. Picking our way through the bric-a-brac and treasures, Bruce hummed in anticipation while I sneezed.

"Eureka, Tish! Paintings and more paintings!" Bruce must have looked at a dozen assorted pictures before he whooped, "Got it!" He pulled out a dusty canvas. And another. "This is it, Tish — two beauts."

The first, and smaller, painting was of a beady-eyed Scottie that was barely distinguishable from a background of dark pines. When Bruce turned the other canvas around for me to see, I knew he'd found the painting I'd remembered. Through the spiderwebs and dirt I could make out two dogs. I guessed they were terriers, though all one could see of the dog in the background was its rear end and tail. Its top half was invisible and presumably in some poor creature's burrow. The dog in the foreground, an interested observer, stood in profile.

"The frame is perfect, isn't it, Tish? Can't we just clean up the painting and maybe wash off the dirt — or whatever you do?"

"Whatever you do" was apt. Once I'd cleaned a century-old painting of a cowboy and an Indian by swabbing it with cotton soaked in alcohol; the process was so successful, I uncovered a whole other Indian. But using the same technique on an old still life of bottles and fruit had removed most of the subject matter, so I wasn't exactly confident about my skill as a restorer.

Bruce was right about the frame; it was perfect, though it needed attention. That didn't present a problem. A little plastic wood here and there, some paint right off my palette, then a little wax or some varnish — Bruce could probably sell the painting for the frame alone.

My descent from the loft was more graceful than my ascent up the ladder, which I could never have managed without Bruce's hand firmly planted on my fanny. Safely on the ground, I untangled the paintings from a rope hammock Bruce had cleverly used to lower our loot.

Practically giddy with our success, Bruce and I carried our treasures back to the house.

Hilary was frowning at his watch and didn't ask anything about our search. No: Did we have any luck? No: Could he see the paintings? No, he just frowned at his watch as though that's all he'd been doing since we last saw him and finally asked, "Are we ready?"

I laughed and did what was expected of me — I made room for Hilary's breakfast party. I pushed books, papers, binoculars, rowboat-sized carpet slippers, an umbrella, and the cat, Vanessa, to the other end of his mile-long refectory table. I accomplished this just in time for Hilary to put down his elegant copper chafing dish.

"Light it," he said.

I patted a fake yawn and handed the matches to Bruce, "Here, boy, your godfather wants a fire. I can assure you that only when the chef, here, is going through a culinary spasm do I tolerate his arrogance. I do it for reasons of compassion and a regard for his health."

It was quite a show the old maestro put on. With the dexterity of a magician, Hilary poured batter into the sizzling pan. Seconds later he flipped the crêpe to brown both sides, then with another flip landed the open crêpe on one of our hot plates. Next a bowl of sliced peaches went into the frying pan with brown sugar and Calvados. With a twist of the wrist, Hilary ignited the brandy into a billow of flame, Vanessa leaped off the table, Bruce clapped his hands, and I was once again reminded of what a super hostess friend of mine says: "When in doubt, set it on fire."

Hilary folded each crêpe over a mound of peaches and added a dollop of sour cream and a pinch of nutmeg. We groaned with pleasure. Hilary, finally relaxed and happy, fingered one singed eyebrow as he accepted our accolades.

Friends marvel that such epicurean feasts can be produced in Hilary's hellhole of a kitchen. The place is a maze of wired machines and gadgets and dangling, clanging pots and pans. Instead of cool, handsome Hilary, one expects to see the devil himself dancing around, exhaling smoke and fire and stirring the pot with a lethal fork.

Not until Hilary brought in cups of espresso did he ask about the results of our trip to the barn.

Bruce blew dust off the paintings with his brandy-laden breath, and I must say, even with bare canvas where one dog's hindquarters should be, they looked pretty good when he put them up on the mantle.

"There you are, Tish," Hilary said. "Easy

as pie, nothing to it. Just clean 'em up, and Bruce here will be the king of the concessionaires."

"Easy as pie, we'll see." The brandied peaches had softened me from head to toe, so instead of carrying on about how really difficult it would be — my valuable time, and all that — I said I'd look them over in my studio and pronounce my verdict later. "But right now, I want to see that monster van of yours."

That was not to be. Bruce said he had to rush off to New Hampshire to set up for tomorrow's dog show.

I refused Hil's offer to come over later to cook dinner for us. A single gastronomic orgy was enough for one day. I probably wouldn't sober up till noon, and I still had to recoup from doing the boogie, plus the promise I'd made to myself to clean the studio.

Never have I offered to help Hilary clean up after a party or one of his special meals. I know I wouldn't be able to stop, and that isn't how I want to spend the rest of my allotted time on this earth. Maintaining the status quo, I bade Hilary and Bruce farewell and walked home, Lulu trotting at my heels while I carried the paintings wrapped in brown paper.

My living room is as serene as Hil's is cha-otic. I favor warm colors. My draperies are marmalade; my Kashmir rug, mixed beige, gray, and tangerine. I'm a sucker for the gleam of polished brass and especially fancy the lead-crystal decanters on my bar. A hor-izontal gold mirror over the mantle lets you look into what was Doug's study. The tiny room is lined with books, a leather Morris chair is beside the telephone, and the yank-out bed is covered in an Indian print.

You have to walk through my cheerful yellow kitchen to reach the studio, added on to the back of the house when we moved to Vermont about twenty years ago. It's my idea of heaven.

I closed the door. My friends have the habit of calling or yoo-hooing at the front door and walking right in. However, no one barges into the studio without an invitation, thank goodness. I had pledged both Bruce and Hilary to silence about my role in Oper-ation Dog Painting.

I unwrapped the paintings, and after care-fully using my vacuum cleaner on both of them, I put the Scottie aside. If the terriers responded to treatment, I might clean the Scottie, but for the moment I slid that canvas into my painting rack.

I toyed with the idea of removing the

black-and-white terrier's canvas from the wooden stretchers but decided on a simpler method: building up the back of the canvas, between the stretchers, with layers of cardboard so that I'd be able to press on and poke at the painting without making dents, or worse, holes.

I cleaned a magnifying glass on my shirttail as I thought about the artist's signature. If whoever it was was anything like me, he or she signed the painting as an afterthought and frequently with thin paint, which made printing easier.

Propping the painting on my easel, I studied it with the aid of the magnifying glass. In the right-hand corner I could make out a few letters, but there was nothing resembling a name. I decided to leave that part of the picture untouched.

What I needed, I mused, was a book I'd read about called *The Forger's Handbook*. I'd have to ask Millie if she could track it down for me. Or would consulting such a book be an admission I'd rather not think about?

I wondered just how common art forgery was. One doesn't hear about it often, probably because no one wants to admit having been taken in by a fake. For dealers, admitting to poor judgment isn't good business and might undermine the buying public's faith in their offerings. Any walk through a museum reveals students busily copying the old and not-so-old masters. If I remember correctly from art school days, the activity was encouraged, but the rule was that no copy should be the exact size of the original painting.

Often I've refinished frames and have made them look old — called antiquing — with the help of an ice pick to create wormholes and a stippling brush for fly specks. It's not hard to imagine that some of the museum copies were given the same treatment and passed off as the real McCoy.

"Oh, my God!" I leaped off my stool and in so doing nudged the painting off the easel. I just caught it before it hit the sharp corner of my drafting table. I clutched my breast as in an old fashioned vignette of the vapors and stared at the window. "Good God, who are you?"

His face cupped by his hands, a man had his nose pressed against the glass less than a foot away.

I wrenched open the back door and in a red-hot fury rounded the corner of the house. Standing there rubbing the end of his nose was cowboy Jack whatever-his-name-was. It took all my self control not to grab the hoe leaning against the porch railing.

"Sugar," he opened his arms as though to enfold me, "didn't mean to scare you."

With a stiff arm and a flat palm I gave his chest a mighty push. Never have I had such instant satisfaction. The big, boney creature fell ass backward over my wheelbarrow and ended up spread-eagled on the lawn. Lulu, delighted, stood inches from his face, barking.

I scooped the dog up in my arms and went back into the studio, slamming the door behind me and locking it.

I was surprised to find I was shaking. My intention had been to make my annoyance clear to the man, not to do him in. Could I have really injured him? Though he had seemed lithe and wiry last night, he was no spring chicken.

Anger winning out over concern for my fellow man, I left Jack Connors to fend for himself and went into the house.

In the living room I locked the front door. Lulu followed me upstairs where I soaked a wash cloth, wrang it out, then threw myself on the bed, eyes covered, and took deep breaths with long exhalations.

In seconds there was loud knocking on the front door. Lulu flew downstairs to play her noisy role as guardian of the house. Stiff as a plank, I listened to the ruckus for what seemed an eternity. Was my Peeping Tom eager to repay me in kind, or was he going to beseech my forgiveness for his rude intrusion? At least the man could move, walk up porch steps, and use his arms.

Then, thank heavens, he quit. I heard him walk back down the steps. A car door slammed. Lulu was still barking, but I assumed he had departed.

When I finally relaxed, the tiniest bit of remorse crept in. Maybe the clown thought it was perfectly acceptable to press his nose against someone's window. Maybe that's how one behaves wherever he comes from.

Lulu, coming back upstairs, wasn't about to let me collapse like this in the middle of the morning. She walked over me a couple of times as though I were a log, then put her nose within inches of mine to check my condition. Finally I gave up, and, sitting on the side of my bed, I thought about the dogs. Not about Lulu, who was happily prancing around with my wash cloth, but the two paintings in the studio waiting for me.

Of course! I jumped up. My vintage black-and-white Polaroid camera to the rescue. I'd take photographs of the paintings so there could never be any doubt about what I might have added or altered. Bless Dr. Land for inventing the instant camera.

What a boon to those of us who paint portraits; to be able to examine a black-and-white photo of the work in progress is a tremendous help. No longer captivated by color, you can use a black-and-white Polaroid to let you study form and composition.

Back to the studio.

Six

Sitting on the front porch with Lulu, I was admiring the dainty little stack of cucumber sandwiches I was about to eat for lunch.

My thoughts were still in the studio with the paintings I had begun to call "the critters." After recording them with my camera, I had to decide what kind of dogs they were. First look made me think they were smooth- or wire-haired terriers, but then I thought of Jack Russell terriers, the breed that in the last few years has become so popular. Just last week I had read how distressed Prince Charles was to have lost his Jack Russell; all England mourned with him.

A little research was called for. What well-known artist could have painted the critters? Had Jack Russells been invented or named before greats like Edwin Landseer or George Earl? The art world is full of competent and appealing paintings that are unsigned by the artist, and I imagined that that might be especially true of paintings of pets.

Lulu's bark interrupted my musings. I watched a woman emerge from a zillion-dollar motor home. Incorrectly, I refer to all such vehicles as trailers, but this was more like a huge, live-in Cadillac.

My first impression of the lean and lanky woman walking toward me was that she had forgotten to take the hanger out of her denim jacket. She hugged a forest of white geraniums to her chest.

"Oops." She plopped down her load of plants on the porch, grasped Lulu's head between her hands, and planted a noisy kiss on top of her head.

"Jack told me you had a pug. I love them. I'm Jean Connors, and I've come to apologize for my oaf of a husband."

My visitor accepted my invitation to sit down and did so by hiking her fanny up onto the edge of the porch. She spoke in a nasal voice with an inflection that might have originated in Boston.

The khaki T-shirt she wore under her jacket, her slacks, her skin, even her hair, were all the same color. The three cocker spaniels watching us from her trailer were also a part of the yellow-ochre scheme.

I offered her the last triangle of my lunch, which she accepted with enthusiasm.

"Jack thinks cucumber sandwiches are for

sissies, but I adore them. But seriously, Mrs. McWhinny, please accept my peace offering. Jack's behavior can be just awful, but he means no harm, and he's really a dear, generous man, and he's devastated to have upset you so. Here comes himself now."

A truck large enough for a couple of grand pianos pulled up in front of the store. Jack Connors climbed out and walked toward us, holding his Stetson over his heart.

"I hope I'm forgiven. I promise, sugar, I'll never, ever again peek in your windows."

"If you call me sugar one more time, Jack Connors, I'll have to ask Lulu to bite you."

"OK, OK. Yes ma'am, honest, never ever will I call you you-know-what again."

Jean Connors rose and tugged at her husband's sleeve. "Come on, let's leave this poor lady in peace."

I wasn't crazy about "poor lady," either, but I guess the unwelcome events of the morning had let loose the crab in me. There was no excuse for my churlish behavior, so I forced a smile and accompanied them over to the trailer. Lulu watched with disgust as I greeted the wriggling spaniels.

"Home away from home." Jean patted the side of her vehicle. "Inside we have four dog cages, sleeping quarters for two, a head, a stove and fridge, and a generator for the air conditioning and the TV. And Jack's truck, here, holds everything else in the world, including his car."

"You mean to say," I asked, "you live in this . . . in these trucks?"

"No, ma'am, we've rented a place over in Londonderry for the summer. Jean, here, likes to do the dog shows. Last year we were on Long Island, but we really like the mountains."

"My daughter is going to be around these parts so we decided I would do the Northeast shows this year." Jean added that she wished she'd seen Lofton first. "I love little towns with one store."

"Come on, Jeanie — 'member, we got a date for your crate at the garage." Jack laughed at the collection of Lofton dogs who had gathered to check out the spaniels and said, "Do you want to hear them sing?"

Without any encouragement, he threw back his head and howled like a wolf — or was it a coyote? Whatever it was brought the town to a stop. It electrified the dogs, who in a wide range of octaves joined the howling cowboy.

Several villagers rushed out of their houses. My ancient neighbor, Katie, came out on her porch brandishing the frightening gun her husband had carried in the Spanish American war. The choir quit practicing and ran out of the church, whereupon postmaster Charlie, who is also our choirmaster, raised his arms and directed the choir in howling.

Neither Lulu nor I had been part of the chorus, so we slipped away as the racket abated and made our way around to my dinky back porch.

While others make colorful plans for their summer gardens during the winter, my thoughts turn to creating space — shelves, blanket bins, and, in this case, an addition to my porch, which at present was an unlovely catchall. The garbage pail had to go, and I'd replace the two worn chairs and wobbly table to create an inviting place to sit away from the madding crowd. Instead of looking at my favorite street scene, I could court serenity by looking at the trees climbing up Lofty Mountain.

Seated in one of the chairs, I tried to envision the size of my proposed enlargement and considered enclosing the place with screens. Engrossed with mental calculations of square feet and board feet, I gradually became conscious of someone prowling around in my kitchen. It couldn't be Hilary, my usual prowler. He had gone to his dentist in Rutland, and friends usually yoo-hooed at the front door before entering.

The kitchen opened against a jut in the wall, so I couldn't see inside without walking through the doorway. If my visitor turned out to be Jack Connors with another peace offering, I'd murder him.

Inside the kitchen I stood stock still and watched a man removing something from a plastic bag.

"Well," I said.

"Oh, you scared me!" The man waved his hands like a wet chicken. "I'm so sorry. I didn't know you were home."

"Obviously."

The intruder, a slender dark-haired young man, was embarrassed and clearly guilty.

"This is for you." He pointed at a fancy package on the counter. It looked like an old-fashioned bon voyage gift or a lavish present at an office Christmas party.

My memory was being tweaked. "Do I know you?"

"Oh, yes, remember last fall in New York? You were trying to find someone named George. I was the wrong George. I had the flu, and you went out and bought groceries for me and saved my life."

"George, I remember. George what?"

"George Rouse. Sophie said if you weren't home just to put this in your refrigerator. It's a present."

By then George was holding Lulu. This softened me considerably.

"Yoo-hoo. Anyone home?" I knew Sophie's voice.

"Yeah, when I realized who you were, Mrs. McWhinny, I wanted to thank you again."

"What brings you to Lofton? Surely you didn't come all this way to put something in my ice box."

"He's staying with me," Sophie said. Sometimes I seem to be able to learn more by just being quiet. So I waited. "He's a friend of Kim's." I guess I looked blank. "You know, the friend I told you is coming to stay with me, remember? Kim, the one who likes to sand things? Didn't I tell you? She's Bruce's daughter."

"No, you didn't. I couldn't be more surprised."

I asked George, "Has Sophie enlisted you to work on the house, too?"

"Oh, sure, I want to help, but I'm really here doing a paper for my MBA."

Now I remembered the whole scene. Me barging in on George in his messy little Greenwich Village apartment. At the time he thought I was from the Department of Health or some such because he obeyed instantly when I told him to shape up, to shower and shave, and I'd return with proper food — which I did — and we had a brief visit. And I do remember his saying he'd put something good in my cupboard some day. I remember thinking that although sickly, what a nice young man he was.

A look at Sophie told me that she shared my opinion. If her friend who sanded thought of George Rouse as her very own cup of tea, I could envision a rough scenario ahead.

The kids watched me exclaim with joy at the bouquet of fattening, expensive goodies packed in a basket from one of Manchester's many epicurean stores. I kissed the jar of Beluga caviar and thanked George for the crock of paté de foie gras. Hilary would be overjoyed to see a can of shad roe he swore had vanished from the marketplace. I groaned with pleasure at another crockful of Stilton cheese as I visualized the wildly swinging needle on my treacherous bathroom scale. "I thank you. Hilary thanks you. Even Lulu thanks you."

Sophie laughed. "Anymore thank yous and we won't get any work done," she said and herded George out of my house.

As they left, I saw them pause to speak to weeny Lily Blount, who was headed my way.

It was too late and too rude to duck out of sight, so I greeted her warmly.

"For you, Mrs. McWhinny, pumpkin bread. It's about the only thing I can make. I hope you like it."

"I do, I do. Sit down and tell me how things are going."

Her dog, Whiskers, jumped up on the porch and made circles with Lulu.

Kate Westervelt's clothes had made a difference in Lily's appearance. Jeans, sneakers and a plaid flannel shirt helped to erase her anemic look, and the delicious smell of warm bread overwhelmed my previous impression of tired eau de Bloomingdale's.

"Has Jeremy got his camera on the ready? The weatherman tells me the weekend will be beautiful."

"Yes, he has — we've decided to go to a dog show; I've forgotten where."

"You're going to show Whiskers?"

"You're kidding, Whiskers? Naw, I'm just going to show her the other dogs. Jeremy will take pictures. He thinks he can sell them as a series."

"How long have you and Jeremy been married?"

Thought I might as well dig out some of the facts that our committee missed. If Lily said they'd been married for more than six months, the guy should be in jail for cradle snatching.

"Married?" She nibbled on an already well-nibbled fingernail. "Let's see, since after Christmas, yeah, after Christmas."

Would a new bride be in such doubt about her wedding date? Even with a failing memory, I have no trouble remembering when I married Doug. "Did you dash off to the justice of the peace or have a bang-up affair?"

"We got married at home."

"And where is home?" I could tell I'd gone too far. Crossed the line beyond friendly interest to nosiness. "I mean, if Jeremy told us where you both came from, I've forgotten. Now, I was born and brought up in New York City."

"That's nice. I gotta go. Jeremy will wonder where I am. Come on, Whiskers." She hurried back down the walk and across to the store.

Watching her go, I said to myself, aside from sex, what in the world could those two have in common? I wondered if we'd been too quick to accept them for the job. Had Jeremy's charm robbed us of our wits and made me ignore his fragile partner? And what did he have in his briefcase?

Maybe under that bloodless exterior Lily was tough, dancer tough. Sophie had already begun to call Lily "Lolita," an appropriate but unfortunate name that I'm sure would catch on all too easily.

Oh, well, what could happen during their trial period? For ten hours a day, five days a week, they were under the constant scrutiny of everyone in Lofton and dozens of others.

Hilary had persuaded me that my imagination had been working overtime when I suspected Jeremy of trying to do me in with a tower of tuna and corned beef hash. But then Hil really seemed to like our storekeeper and really disliked the way I teased him when he expressed the naive thought that Jeremy's role in Lily's life was avuncular if not paternal. Her husband?

I watched her leave with the strong sensation that there was more to learn about the waif — about them both. Not that I cared, but Lily's visit firmed up my resolution to enlarge the back porch. I didn't want to spend so much time in their front yard. In Lofton's front yard.

Seven

The rest of the day was shot. I blamed it on the morning's invasions, but the truth of the matter is I was stiff and sore from my merry antics on the dance floor the previous night.

Hilary called in a foul mood. His dentist had announced that Hil needed a root canal and had to have an aged tooth recapped, urging him to get both jobs done as soon as possible. Hilary said he refused to share his grumpiness with me. Besides, he said, who wants to sit around and watch someone take Tylenol?

We agreed to have dinner at the end of the week.

For the next few days I worked on the critters. It was the kind of painstaking work I like to avoid, but I had to admit it was kind of fun.

I had a brainstorm and spent half an hour painting my name, Tish, upside down, in the hairs of the burrowing terrier's tail. I regarded it as added insurance the picture couldn't be passed off as a Rembrandt or whoever it was balmy Bruce had in mind.

Hilary called Friday morning to say that Bruce wanted the painting. The Bennington dog show was the next day, and he thought it would be the perfect time to display what he called "our" painting.

"Tell Bruce he can have the painting, but it's still wet and he'll have to treat it tenderly," I said. "But more important, Hil, impress upon your dear godchild that if he says one word to anyone about my role in this, I'll have his scalp. Yours, too. Promise?"

"Who would I tell?"

I loathed that particular response when I've told someone a secret. Who? He could tell anyone at all. They'd love it and tell everyone they met for the next two weeks.

"I mean it Hil, tell no one, not even Sophie."

He promised.

When I put down the phone, I picked up my powerful magnifying glass and zeroed in on the area where a signature might naturally be found on a painting. Even under strong light there was no way I could translate a few vertical marks into letters.

The heck with it, I thought. That's Bruce's concern. There were hundreds of paintings attributed to the school of such and such an artist. He'd have to name the painting, too. There was no date and no definitive marks on the back of the stretchers nor on the canvas.

The critters had been underpainted, which means the figures were built up in layers of egg tempera. This mixture, made with an egg and equal parts oil and water, is then applied to the subject with a brush dipped in the tempera and mixed with powdered white. The artist builds almost a bas-relief with the tempera alternated with oil and oil-color glazes so that with luck, your painting may retain the glow of the old masters.

The critters had had a hard life. Parts of the old tempera had cracked, and where the standing terrier's hindquarters should have been, the canvas was bare.

Reinventing the pooch's backside wasn't difficult, but it had taken a long time to allow the tempera to dry before applying the color glazes.

In all modesty, my handiwork looked pretty darn good. I was torn between embarrassment at what I was doing and pleasure at my dexterity.

Placing the canvas flat on the floor, I sprayed it with varnish, hoping to make the old and new parts of the picture look uniform. I realized that varnish on wet paint wasn't a good idea because it would take at least twenty-four hours or more to dry. Again, that was Bruce's problem. I decided not to fiddle with the frame. It needed a professional touch. Besides, its obvious age would enhance the value of the painting.

With my work complete, I went to reward myself with a long, hot soak. Almost totally submerged in the bathtub, I pried the daily allotment of paint out from under my nails and gave them a good scrubbing. The only time my hands look ladylike is when I'm on a vacation or after the occasional manicure.

When the bathwater started to cool, I forced myself to vacate the tub. In the bedroom, Lulu's soulful eyes watched me pull on black slacks, slide into suede slippers, and button the frogs on my mandarin shirt. She snoozed when I was in the tub, but it made her nervous to see me get dressed. There was always the awful possibility that I might be going out for dinner without her. I brushed my hair, put on pearl earrings and made a couple of passes at my face. Giving myself the onceover in my wonderful cheval glass that made me look thin, I said the magic words, "You're coming, Lulu."

Lulu performed her version of the highland fling while I pulled my Irish mink (a mohair stole) out of the closet. Ahead of time as usual, we set off for Hilary's house.

"Tish. You can't believe how glad I am to see you." Hilary gave me a huge hug. "I'm so sick of looking at my dentist's fat neck, I can hardly stand it."

From Hilary that was love talk.

Around his tweedy arm I saw the table was set for five. "We're five for dinner?"

"Yup. Invited Sophie and her guest. Some fella, she said. Have you met him?" He didn't let me reply. "Is he serious?"

"Oh, Hil, relax, he's probably her podiatrist. Where's Bruce?"

"Primping in my room. You didn't see his van — no, it's parked in back."

Bruce bounced into the room just as Sophie and George Rouse came in the front door. There was a flurry of handshakes and hugs.

Hilary asked Sophie to take care of the drinks because he had to go out to tend the charcoal grill.

Just as he turned to leave, the front door opened, and two extra-large golden retrievers loped into the room. They were followed by a tiny person shouting unheeded commands. "Sit!" she yelled, "Sit!" Both dogs jumped on the couch and sat wiggling and panting with joy at the wonder of themselves.

"Down, Donder, down, Blitzen." She suddenly dropped her shoulder bag on the floor and then threw herself into Bruce's arms. "Daddy!"

We all watched the familial scene with bemusement.

"How did you find me?" Bruce asked the tangled mop of hair below his chin.

"Sophie left me a note and said I should come here." She turned her crisp little dime-sized face to Hilary. "You must be Uncle Hilary. I'm sorry about the dogs."

Hilary seemed amused. It was fortunate Bruce's daughter hadn't arrived after Hilary had started to cook on the grill, or worse, served dinner, or her reception would have been less gracious.

"George!" Kim made George's name last like the line of a song. "Oh, George!" She stretched her arms wide and trapped his arms to his side in a gigantic hug. She kissed his Adam's apple.

Sophie's bared teeth in no way resembled a smile.

It was my turn to meet Kim. Her face made me think of a sparrow's egg in a hawk's nest. I could have drawn her features in horizontal lines. For one so tiny she struck me as quite intimidating. However, her mellow dogs told a different story.

We settled down with assorted drinks to listen to Kim. She was so very sorry she hadn't kept up with Dad just lately but was delighted to know they'd both be doing the New England dog show circuit. Did Dad know that her divorce from Lester Nolan had become final? And, she said, rubbing her thumb and index finger together, did he know that she'd gotten her "pound of flesh"?

This was sweet Bruce's daughter? A quick glance from Hilary told me our reactions were similar.

George looked a little embarrassed and had edged away to massage a dog's ear.

Sophie stood with a glass of wine in one hand and her other on her hip. One of her thick, dark eyebrows was raised, giving the impression of sophisticated cynicism. Breeding will out, though, so she did manage to convey welcoming banalities to Kim and ask if she'd had trouble finding us.

"No. I asked the guy at the store. He's cool. He loved the dogs. Said he's a photographer. Told me the only way to get a good picture of a dog is on your knees. Maybe tomorrow I'll find out what he charges."

Hilary left the room, followed by Kim's

dogs and Lulu. I rummaged around in the sideboard to extract more napkins and then set another place for Kim.

Each time Bruce seemed about to speak to me, I frowned and shook my head. I didn't know if Hil had passed on my threat, and I was afraid his tongue might have been loosened by Hilary's heavy hand with the booze and he'd let the whole group in on our little secret.

Sophie had vanished to help Hilary, and in no time we were transported by floating aromas and the sight of Sophie bearing a gigantic bowl — more like a washtub — full of spareribs. Hilary followed with another container of his special cole slaw. Next came a platter of sautéed sweet potatoes, and I was glad that I remembered the finger bowls.

"Here you are, young fella." Hilary pushed a bottle of Burgundy and another of beer close to George. "Why don't you do the honors?" Then in the worst Texas accent you ever heard, Hil invited us to dig in.

I don't know what most people do to spareribs, but I know Hilary simmers his for almost an hour before preparing them for the grill. We groaned, purred, and growled. On the couch the dogs salivated.

I stopped gorging long enough to look at Kim. Her dinner plate supported a little pile of cole slaw, nothing else.

"No spareribs?"

"No. I don't eat meat."

"Oh, too bad. The sweet potatoes are yummy, try them."

"Thanks just the same, no fried food."

"Well, at least I'm glad there's plenty of cole slaw for you."

She poked at it with her fork. Damned if I'd ask her if she did or didn't like cole slaw. Sophie saw Kim's plight and slipped into the kitchen, producing a plate of bread and butter, a few stalks of celery, and some ripe olives.

When our first attack on the spareribs subsided, Hilary turned his attention to George, asking what he planned to do in Vermont.

George said he had to write a paper for his MBA, it was to be about Vermont's first millionaire.

That grabbed everyone's interest.

Hilary was delighted that someone Sophie might favor had a down-to-earth interest in something as prosaic as making money.

"And who might this millionaire be?"

"Silas Griffith. A wily, industrious lumber tycoon from Danby."

"Never heard of him."

"Well, he was quite a man. Had as many

as thirty brick kilos on the mountains. A lot of them were on Mt. Tabor. He converted over a hundred cords of wood into charcoal each month. He used hundreds of horses and had eighty oxen of his own. As a matter of fact, in the eighteen eighties Griffith owned a farm over in Landgrove and ran a boardinghouse for his farriers, teamsters, and loggers."

"Wow," Sophie said. "Way to go. Nowadays you're supposed to be extra smart and sit in an office or on your yacht and let someone else do the work."

"I want to hear more about him." Hilary beamed. "Where are you getting your MBA?"

"Harvard," Kim said. "He's getting it at Harvard."

"Good for you. You were an undergraduate there, too?"

"No," Kim said, "he went to Williams."

George didn't look at Kim, but I could tell from the twitch in his jaw that he was annoyed and I guessed for some reason muzzled.

"Yeah," he said, "Williams."

I wondered if George had a special appeal for strong women. I had taken him over for a brief half hour in New York, Sophie obviously liked him, and Kim acted as if she owned him.

"I thought you were going to ask me if I wasn't a little old to be getting my MBA. I am." George smiled. "I had a variety of other jobs for a few years after college. Blind alleys. Then I decided to go for it."

"Don't see how you can go wrong," Hilary said. "Can't have too many arrows in your quiver."

"Raise your hands if you want dessert," Sophie said, abruptly changing subjects. "It's coffee ice cream, and I'm going to dish it up in the kitchen."

I was gratified to see that Kim raised her hand and also jumped to her feet to help Sophie clear the table.

George had moved back from the table. I imagined he was trying to work his way out of the limelight because he was embarrassed to have Kim speaking for him. I remember how I hated it when I was young whenever a current beau acted possessive about me. I mean, gosh, you don't want to scare off the competition.

The ice cream arrived, carried on a tray by Sophie and parceled out by Kim. Hilary took a silver bowl of shredded bitter chocolate from the sideboard and, deftly wielding tongs, put a generous plenty on each serving.

Bruce was the first to quit the table.

"Tish, give me the pleasure of driving you home. I'm going directly from here to Bennington."

"For the dog show tomorrow, I presume."

"You bet. I'm so glad you'll be there, Kim." He patted his daughter's shoulder. "We'll have some fun. I certainly hope all the rest of you are coming."

"Can't you go in the morning, Dad?"

"No way. It takes me at least five hours to set things up. You know, the awning, tables and racks . . . it's quite a job. I'll do some of it tonight and the rest tomorrow morning." Bruce winked at me. "Like hanging pictures."

Oh, dear. I had a deep conviction that nothing good ever came from a wink.

Kim put her arm around her father's waist. "Have you got any paintings of dogs, Dad?"

"I have a real beaut, an old master, you wait and see."

"You do?" Kim said. "I hope it's the real thing. Did you read about the guy who was a whiz at forging paintings who's going to have the book thrown at him — what was it? Five years in jail?"

George laughed, "Maybe he can make a mint painting portraits of other inmates."

Bruce closed his eyes. Hilary looked at the

floor. I raised my gaze to heaven where I prayed the god or goddess of fixer-uppers was receiving my message.

Eight

When I phoned Sophie, she answered the phone she recently had installed in the barn. She said she was cleaning the goats' chambers and would join us at the dog show in the afternoon. In response to my question, she said Kim had left hours ago. "Those poor dogs," she said. "Kim doesn't feed them the day of the show so that they'll roll over, shake hands, or do whatever they're supposed to do for treats or yummies." George, she said, would show up after a visit to the Danby library.

Hilary was disappointed. He loved to create grand picnics for friends but had the sense to know he'd go mad if no one appeared at the exact moment he was ready to serve. He had to settle for his usual role of providing glorious food for two.

Me, I was experiencing a combination of excitement over the outing and trepidation over the painting. The post office is right across from my house. Charlie is thoughtful and kind about looking in on Lulu when I plan to be out for more than a couple of hours. Today Charlie said he'd send his dog, Luke, over to sit with Lulu and promised to check on them often.

With Lulu's welfare seen to, we piled into my Isuzu for the ride to Bennington.

At the end of our drive, Hilary said that given Bruce's gentle nature, he was surprised that his daughter, Kim, was such a preemptive young person — and wondered why George put up with it. "I wouldn't," he said. Before I could reply, Hilary started to rave about George, who he thought might at long last be an acceptable suitor for Sophie.

"You don't get it, dear," I interrupted. "Kim is number one. Kim is the reason George came to Lofton. Not to put goodies in my fridge, but to be with Kim. Didn't you notice Sophie's grimace when Kim got that midsection grip on George last night? Sophie took a major shine to George at the dance. You saw them."

"I thought Sophie was very nice to Kim. I mean, they're friends."

"Let's say she was polite. Hey, here we are."

We drove into the parking lot by a line of portable toilets and were instantly in dogland.

Dogs in cars barked. Dogs leaped in, out, and around vans. A little boy ran in circles with a huge German shepherd. His younger sister was hugging a chow. Their mother was weaving her way toward the fairgrounds with a little furry creature under her arm. I recognized the Blounts' Mercedes with Whiskers's head sticking out the window.

Another parking lot closer to the action was crammed with monster RVs, many of them larger and grander than Jean Connors's. There were all kinds of trailers, vans, trucks, and station wagons. Most of them had rigged-up attached awnings so that the dogs and their retinues could escape the sun — or rain.

I had asked Kim the night before what happened to a dog show in case of rain.

"You get wet," she said.

We guessed that the next ring of vehicles between us and two large tents must belong to the concessionaires.

Hilary paused to count them. "Twelve," he said. "Probably more; I can't see from here."

We spotted Bruce's green-striped awning, but because his space was full of people, we pushed on and entered the rear tent, which turned out to be the largest beauty parlor I've ever seen.

What a racket! And only some of the noise was contributed by barking dogs. More pervasive was the sound of hair dryers, the buzz of clippers, and the whirr of oscillating fans.

There were boxes on crates, boards on cages, and high stools where long-suffering beasts stood patiently, being transformed into beauty contestants.

I must have said as much to Hil because a woman beside us said, "That's what this is — a damn beauty contest." She removed a cigarette butt from her mouth. "Here I have the best damn retriever in the world, and what's he gonna do? Be in a beauty contest." Hilary took the dog's proffered paw. "That's his trouble — isn't it, Travis? — he always wants to shake hands with the judge."

Beyond Travis, we walked by a tower of cages and into the midst of a covey of Malteses. I had to laugh at Hilary. He looked like an angel, or possibly God, rising out of a heavenly cloud — a cloud created by half a dozen fluffy white dogs sniffing his boots.

The other tent, which was quiet compared to the beauty parlor bedlam, contained two separate rings. A group of beagles was leaving the far one. In the other, I was surprised to see ten or twelve dogs of different breeds, unattended, lying in a large circle.

"Where are their owners?" Hilary asked a

large woman clutching a Chihuahua to her breast.

"It's an obedience class. Scarlett, here, could never make it. She can't bear to have me two inches away from her."

I heard Jean Connors's unmistakable voice calling my name. "Over here, Mrs. McWhinny! Over here!" She was seated at ringside, where she patted the camp chair beside her and beckoned.

I nudged Hilary, pointed at Jean, and left him stroking Scarlett with his index finger and chatting up Big Mom.

I assessed Jean's appearance with a tinge of envy. Her blue blazer looked perfect with her flat chest. Her gray slacks were tailor-made, and the alligator loafers she wore must have cost a bundle.

"Have you shown your dogs yet?"

"Nope. I had to back out. Both Priscilla and Macho had the trots this morning, and I didn't want to take a chance on giving or getting any bugs. And I rarely show my prize bitch, Queen Bee, any more. Actually, it's kind of pleasant just being a spectator for a change. Oh, look" — Jean stood up — "there's Kim. Said she met you last night at Hilary Oats's. Oh, good, she's showing Blitzen. It's a big class. Let's cross our fingers."

Speaking of fingers, I noticed how incongruous the bonbon-sized diamond Jean sported looked with her seriously bitten nails.

We watched a dozen or more golden retrievers enter the ring. I had a moment of thanks that I didn't have to choose just one from such a gorgeous group of dogs.

"She won't win," Jean said. "The judge likes smaller goldens. But I am glad Kim is dressed properly."

"She looks great."

"I mean that peacock blue really sets off Blitzen's coat. See the handler with khaki slacks? A no-no. Too close in color to his dog. Kim used to revolt against such ploys to enhance the animal. Glad she's learned."

"Do you ever show dogs together?"

"Lordy, yes. Kim was showing dogs in the AKC juniors when she was eleven."

"Is Jack here? Does he like all this?"

"Sometimes he comes to shoot the breeze with some friends. But he doesn't last long. He was here earlier. He may have gone. Look — Hilary is trying to get your attention. Seems to want you over there. Don't let him get away before I have a chance to say hello. And" — she put her hand on my arm as I was rising — "don't miss seeing Bruce's new old painting. It's awesome.

Lord knows where he got it."

Awesome. The word made me apprehensive. I mumbled good-byes and darted around the ring to grab Hilary's elbow.

"Jean says Bruce's new painting is 'awesome'."

"Awesome." Hilary shrugged. "Kids use the word all the time — probably for anything except an object that inspires awe. Got something to show you."

He led me to a prominent vendor's tent. He grinned. "Awesome, isn't it?"

Dogs — all kinds, sizes and shapes of dogs — were painted on every imaginable object. Dogs' heads on clocks, mugs and candlesticks. Dogs on aprons, placemats, hankies, and ties. There were tiny dogs painted on pins, earrings, and brooches. Caps, shirts, socks, and mittens all sported dogs. Large dogs adorned slabs of slate or sliced tree trunks and marble tombstones.

Hilary was carried away. "Look at that collie. And that setter on the toilet seat — and look at the airedale; he's perfect. Tish, if I'd known about this artist, I'd never have bothered you about Bruce's painting. I wonder why Bruce didn't get this artist to paint an old master for him?"

I knew why Bruce hadn't asked his fellow concessionaire to paint a portrait for him.

He'd have had to pay for it!

That was an uncharitable thought, I knew I didn't really believe Bruce was a freeloader, but like the abbé in a novel by Stendhal, Bruce sinned so naturally, you could hardly call it sinning.

"Excuse me." Hilary spoke to a tense young woman chewing a pencil and rearranging a display. "Are you the artist?"

"No, just minding the store." She pointed. "There he is, Phil Tune, with the man in the red shirt."

The red shirt belonged to George Rouse. I wondered if George was taking Tune to see Bruce's awesome painting.

We followed the pair to Bruce's place, but the distance of fifty feet took at least ten minutes. We had to navigate our way around dogs going in three directions, and we stopped to greet other creatures that were firmly planted in the middle of the pathway with the obvious intention of greeting fellow contestants as well as their audience.

They were the gregarious ones, eager to be patted — warm-eyed hounds, a drooling St. Bernard, and an especially huggable Wheaten.

A massive brindle bulldog stopped to give me a piercing look. I had a moment of thinking we might have met before. A Burmese mountain dog stood on my right foot and raised his soulful eyes to engage mine. An English sheepdog shook his head to get a better look at me.

"Hil, do you think I might have been a dog in some other life?"

"That's possible." He thought a minute. "Yes, I imagine you were a terrier — the type of terrier that likes to corner rats."

"Ugh, thanks a lot. I'd rather have been something svelte like a saluki or an afghan. You, Hil, were a Great Dane — that's a given."

"No, I'd never have made it through the Ice Age without a fur coat. How about a Newfoundland?"

We ceased our ancestral musings as we neared the green-striped awning.

Bruce, flushed and beaming, was shaking a blond man's hand with both of his. I had a feeling he'd been doing it for a while.

"Hilary!" Bruce called. "Tish, come! I want you to meet Leland Shaw."

Even from twenty feet and with iffy eyesight, I could see that Leland Shaw wore a rug. That, or he had tried a home dye job. It looked as though he'd upgraded his front teeth, too. They were too perfect to be true. I could just hear Sophie scolding me for being so critical — but she'd get a chuckle out of his fancy clothes. A paisley ascot was tucked into his shirt collar. His jacket was open to show off the baby-blue braces that held up his linen slacks.

Bruce — no sartorial slouch himself with khaki pants, a blue blazer, and a polka dot tie — said, "I know you've been to Lee's gallery, Tish. Quadruped Gallery in Woodstock. You know, right there on the main street."

I tried to imagine him with dark hair — or no hair — or with ordinary teeth but couldn't remember the man. He professed to be ecstatic at our meeting and gave me that double-handed shake that seemed to be popular today.

"Have you seen Bruce's painting, Mrs. McWhinny? It's awesome — really awesome." Lying, I of course denied having seen it. For the first time, I began to have doubts that this awesome painting was of the same critters that I patched up during the week.

"I've seen your paintings often and have wished I could persuade you to do portraits of animals." Shaw cocked his head. "Perhaps you'd consider it? It should be more fun than painting people. Dogs and cats can't complain."

After more chitchat, Leland was engaged

by yet another friend, so I inched away to join the group under the striped awning.

It was too crowded to take in all of Bruce's knick-knacks and artifacts. Beyond all the heads and shoulders I could see paintings and prints hung against a burlap background on the side of his long RV.

I felt Hil behind me, and he pushed us into the front row.

I was speechless. The burrowing critter and his standing friend were given the center position and hung at eye level, and clear to all, in the lower right hand corner of the painting, was a signature: Landseer.

I could feel Hil's heart beating behind my head. I was torn between screaming, attacking Bruce, or passing out.

On a profound exhalation, Hilary said, "How could he?"

Nine

Aghast, we were still standing in front of the painting in silence when Bruce came up behind and between us and put an arm around each of our waists.

"I'll bet you're surprised. It's unbelievable, isn't it? There it was all the time, Landseer's signature."

Still twitching with anger, I didn't trust myself to speak.

"Bruce" — Hilary cleared his throat — "I don't know what to say. I'm shocked that you would do such a thing. You must realize that you could get in serious trouble forging a name, particularly a name with monetary value."

"Do such a thing!" Bruce faced Hilary. "All I did was rub the paint on that corner where you'd expect to see a signature, and there it was: Landseer."

"You rubbed it," I asked acidly, "with what?"

"Just a wad of cotton soaked in gin. Isn't it

astonishing?" Bruce clapped his hands. "As Lee says, It's awesome."

I didn't believe Bruce, and I'd heard that word "awesome" once too often. "You'll have to excuse me. I may go vomit."

Bruce grabbed my arm as I turned to leave, but I shrugged off his hand and walked away.

Mindlessly I walked by vendors' tents that sold books, custom T-shirts, dog foods and bed and blankets, and Lord knows what all. I wasn't really looking at them.

"If you were a dog, lady, I'd take a picture of you."

It took me a minute to get off the thunderous cloud I was on to recognize Jeremy Blount.

"I saw you and Mr. Oats in the tent with that Landseer painting. Have you any idea what he wants for it?"

I shook my head. "Go ask Hilary," I said bitterly. "Or better, Bruce Hemphill. He owns it."

If Jeremy had more to say, I didn't hear it. I finger wiggled a wave and sidled away to sort out my tangled thoughts.

If Bruce was so deceitful that he had forged Landseer's name, it was foolish to think he would stick to his word about not selling the painting. I could picture the scenario: Bruce pocketing a huge check. The buyer for some reason becomes suspicious, has the painting analyzed at the Met, and finds that it's a fake. The law descends on Bruce, and he tells all. And who knows? He might even blame the spurious signature on me.

What a fool I was. Every morning as regularly as two deep knee bends and brushing my teeth, I should practice saying NO out loud ten times.

This was all my own damned fault. I eased into a vacant chair and tried out some excuses and explanations that I might offer to the jury. I didn't really expect to be led to the gallows for painting one pooch's rear end, it was the *sub rosa* aura that bothered me. I'd rather brag openly about the good job I'd done than have to silently watch Bruce pass the painting off as a Landseer.

Like Lulu, I get kissed on the top of the head more than most people I know. For one reason, I'm five-two and am surrounded by tall people; and another is that I see no advantage to standing up when you can sit down. Martha Graham once said that she only sat down if she couldn't lie down.

This kisser was Sophie, who looked quite jazzy in gray linen shorts, a striped tank top, and a multicolored straw hat. She said she had only been at the show for ten minutes, and the hot news was Bruce Hemphill's Landseer. She wondered if I had seen it yet.

Oh, Lord, what would Sophie think of me if she knew my role in the Landseer drama? I got to my feet, took a deep breath, squared my shoulders, and gave myself a private lecture; Snap out of it, kid. Forget the painting. Let fate have its way and the hell with it.

Happily, Sophie dropped the topic and pointed. "Look at the lousy Brit prick. Kim told me this was going to happen."

"Look at what?"

"The judge. Not only is he over the hill, but he's forgotten he isn't in his jolly old homeland. He's in the U.S. of A."

Sophie and I had different ideas of what over the hill meant; the judge looked well put together to me. "What's wrong with him?"

"He hasn't even looked at Kim's dog. I mean hardly. Blitzen's too big. In England they like small goldens."

Knowing the judge was English may have influenced my thought that he might have stepped out of a PBS Sunday night special. His carriage suggested the military, and his safari-type costume might be his very own antique. He wore a khaki hat and half glasses far down on his straight nose. There was something about his outsized ears that looked familiar.

"What's his name?" Sophie looked at a printout that I guess served as the show's catalogue. "Let's see; oh, here it is. Bixler. Ian Bixler. He's a retired Commander of Her Majesty's Royal Navy. So what's that got to do with dog shows? Gotta go. Told Mrs. Connors I'd bring her a Coke."

Ian Bixler! No wonder those ears looked familiar.

I've always thought old lovers make the best friends, but so far Ian Bixler has been the exception. With my eyes closed, I let the film roll backward for a minute to a time several years after World War II.

My good friend Gordon Grant was a general in the Air Force who had been assigned to duty at the UN in their grand new quarters in New York. I don't remember why, but Gordon borrowed my car, a snazzy Ford Phaeton, and it had the distinction of being the first, possibly the last, car to be stolen from the UN parking lot. Ian Bixler was Gordon's friend and his counterpart representing the British Navy. Just by luck, Ian found my car the next morning parked in front of the Stork Club.

By the end of the week Ian and I were conducting a sizzling affair. We weren't the only dizzy lovers. Everyone was on a high. The town was jumping. My friends accused me of robbing the cradle, but for me that just added to the fun and he wasn't that much younger!

After Ian departed, as wartime lovers do, I didn't see him again for about fifteen years. The occasion was a black-tie opening at the Metropolitan Museum, where I literally ran into him. Champagne glasses in hand (not unusual for us), we stood there grinning at each other while I had to subdue an urge to grab his ears. Before we said a word to each other, a very dressy blonde, who I assumed was his wife, twirled him around and in a rude stage whisper said, "Who is she?" And worse, Ian let himself be led off — but not before I heard him say, "She's nobody, really."

I considered following them to say something equally rude, but Doug and I had just been married, and I didn't think he'd be too pleased to come upon a scene between his new wife and her old beau.

While I hadn't forgotten Ian, I certainly never spent any time remembering him, though my almost total recall made me smile, which is why Hilary found me in a better mood.

"Let's move these chairs back out of the way," I suggested. "Don't want some wolf-hound to insist on sharing our lunch."

We found a quiet spot between two vans with a view of the rings. As we sat down, Hilary said, "You look happier, so I guess you've had time to think, Tish, and to realize that Bruce, bumbler that he is, would never do anything deceitful. It's simply not in his nature." He held up his hand when I opened my mouth to interrupt him. "Now mind you, I realize some of the difficulties. Bruce can't give a reasonable account of the painting's background nor discuss your additions to it without bringing you into the picture."

"Bringing me into the picture? Ha-ha. I don't find all of this very funny, Hil. And sweet as your godchild is, I have no faith in his judgement. Or, let's face it, in him."

"But just listen a minute. Bruce says that Shaw fella might buy it. Then the painting will be his to worry about, and that, my dear, will be the end of that."

"That's what you think, Hilary. But you're forgetting it's not for sale!"

"There you two are!" George Rouse suddenly hunkered down beside us and put a stop to what might have become an over-heated exchange. "Kim wanted me to tell you that Blitzen won a blue and will be in best of the sporting group at about two o'clock in ring one."

"I thought the judge didn't appreciate big goldens," I said.

"That's what everyone said, and the judge kind of ignored Blitz till the very end — and, whammo, gave him the blue."

During this chatter, Hilary — whose interest in dog shows is minimal — had found another chair for George and was passing him bits of paté and stalks of roquefort-stuffed celery. He asked George if he was an old hand at dog shows.

"No," he replied. "My upbringing was so peripatetic that the family could never have animals. Being in the State Department, we never knew where we'd land next. But in spite of being slightly allergic to them, I love dogs. I had an aunt who had a sofa and loveseat and six stuffed chairs in her big old living room, and every seat was always occupied by a dog or a cat. Kim's hoping to teach me to be a handler — a hopeless task."

"I think it's great," Hilary said, passing the bacon and avocado sandwiches, "that you and Kim are helping Sophie work on that house of hers. It will be a good chance for you to get to know Sophie better."

Whoa! For an awful moment I thought

Hil was going to propose to the poor guy, but fortunately a friend of Hilary's pulled him away to meet his companion.

"Was Mr. Oats an actor?" George asked. "I have this feeling I've seen him on the stage or maybe the movies."

"The only role he's ever mentioned was as the cowardly lion in *The Wizard of Oz* in the fourth grade."

Hilary has shrunk, he claims, to six three, but it doesn't detract from his rugged good looks. His big nose, high cheekbones, and the planes and angles of his face could be drawn with a broad marker. Bald friends admire his thick, white hair, and I, for one, am glad he recently shaved off his beard, leaving a dashing, twirlable mustache.

Hilary returned to introduce his friends to me, at which point George excused himself. When Hilary and I were once again alone, I told him I wanted to go back to Bruce's tent.

"I was so upset when I first saw that signature, I didn't really examine the painting. Maybe I can manage it now. And, more important, we'll discuss this business of the critters being for sale."

"Now that Bruce knows it's actually a Landseer, it's different. Why, the painting should bring thousands of dollars. I must say I like the idea of Bruce really succeeding at a venture like this."

"What I want to know is how far this pretense goes. What a farce. And it's my own damned fault for being a part of it."

"What's it worth?"

I realized Hilary had asked the question of Leland Shaw, the super-blond gallery owner who was standing outside Bruce's awning, eating a hot dog.

"It's worth," he replied archly, "whatever someone will pay for it."

Knowing that further eavesdropping would endanger my health, I slithered away and planted myself right in front of the critters. As I studied the picture, I tried to be objective.

I'm Mary Zilch, I told myself, dog lover and a reasonably smart observer. Mary and I agreed it was a damned handsome painting. One dog, presumably one of the first Jack Russell terriers, was poised and still and eloquently attentive. The other terrier's rear end and perky tail should make a viewer eager to see the rest of him and what prey he may have captured. The composition, excellent. The background stayed where it should but was inviting. The frame was an Old-World beauty. Not plaster of paris, but hand carved and probably gilded by some long-gone artisan who practiced the technique of first rubbing a sable paintbrush on his bald head to create static electricity to make the fragile gold leaf adhere to the brush, which he then gently blew onto the prepared surface of the frame.

The signature. I found it impossible to be objective about that. As much as it hurt Hilary to have me call Bruce a liar, I simply couldn't buy his explanation of its unlikely appearance.

"It's wonderful, Tish, just wonderful!" It was Bruce cooing in my ear. "You've really put me on the map."

"Careful there, careful," he then cautioned a man removing the critters painting from the burlap wall. The man was Jeremy Blount.

Jeremy caught my eye and smiled.

"I'm not stealing this, honest I'm not, Mrs. McWhinny. Just want to take a shot of Hemphill, here, with his sensational find."

Jean Connors's la-de-dah voice produced some feeble excuse mes and pardons as she moved in to look at the painting. "See, Ian, there it is. A beaut, isn't it?" She took my arm. "I want you to meet Ian Bixler. He's judging today. He's —"

"Letitia." Ian smiled warmly. "It's been a long time."

We maintained a long handshake, and I responded with equally obvious words. He looked better than I'd remembered from our last encounter. His pink cheeks, sometimes helped along with gin and bitters, looked endearingly familiar. I smiled. His blond hair was gray, but there was plenty of it, and he had the same habit of pinching his lower lip.

"You two have met? Great. I hope we'll all be seeing a lot of each other. Ian is staying at the Lofton Inn."

"You'll be my neighbor," I said.

"I always have been blessed with great good fortune."

"We're lucky to have Ian around this season," Jean said.

"I'm the lucky one," Ian said. "I'm just delighted that the powers that be in dogdom will let an old dinosaur like me point out his favorite pooches. I'm lucky, too, because I have a trumped-up job to locate dog paintings for a client." Ian pointed at the critters, which Jeremy was rehanging. "From here that looks like a dandy."

I wanted to scream. How deep was I going to be mired in this awesome mess?

"We have some serious catching up to do, Tish." Ian looked at his watch. "I'm due in the ring. Ta-ta. See you soon."

Hilary was overjoyed when I told him ta-ta was fine by me, too, that I was tired and eager to get home.

It would be pointless to try to talk to Bruce now with all the hoopla and adulation. Tomorrow, when he was parked at Hilary's, would be soon enough.

Ten

We were just getting into the Isuzu when Bruce came running across the lot, waving his arms.

"Hey, wait up, you guys!" He leaned in the passenger window and panted. "Hey, you promised, Hil, remember?"

"Promised what?"

"You said you'd stay after the show was over. I want you to meet some of my friends. Want to show you off."

"I don't remember making any promises. Tish is tired and we're off." He looked at me. "Right?"

"Whatever plans you've made, please count me out. Why don't you stay, Hil? It might be fun."

"Tish, please," Bruce implored. "I want to have a little party for our painting."

That cinched it. "Forget it, Bruce. I have a pressing engagement, and it's with my bathtub and a particular book."

Bruce held Hilary's arm. "Listen, Hil, just

stay for a little while. I'll drive you home. There'll be a good gang here. Most of us are going to Craftsbury Common tomorrow for a show Monday — so no one is dashing away tonight. Please."

Hilary looked at me as though he expected me to extricate him from the situation. I suppose the look I gave him was heartless, and my remark worse. "This van's leaving." I started the car.

Bruce opened Hilary's door and pulled him outside. I drove away from the scene of a reluctant Hilary being clutched by his beaming godson.

I was being an awful pill. Maybe I should have stayed with Hilary. Bruce and his chums might get too jolly and keep Hil up till all hours, which he'd hate. Possibly all the talk about the awesome painting had siphoned off too many drams of what compassion I had. Ah, well, it was done, and surely Bruce would take good care of his generous, loving godfather.

The thought of my bathtub wasn't really all that compelling, so I decided to take advantage of the fact that I was in Bennington. I found a parking place in front of the bookstore and went in to mosey around.

At the end of the long narrow store I spied Jack Connors. The sign over the shelves his nose was brushing said MYSTERIES. I would have expected to find him under WESTERNS if book stores still have that designation.

The last thing I wanted to do was talk with the man, so I ducked out, having quietly paid for a slim volume of Wallace Stegner's.

Whiskers Blount was the first sight I saw when I made my exit. Her head and paws and half of her body were hanging over the open window of their Mercedes.

My Lord, the dog could fall out! Bennington was no buzzing metropolis, but a dog loose on Main Street? No!

Thank goodness I saw Lily running toward us. She was swinging a paper bag from Dunkin' Donuts. Her offbeat outfit consisted of a glistening silver baseball cap, a black tank top, and white rompers that appeared to be a shorter version of her pasha pants. She put her arm around Whiskers and fed her the rest of her donut.

"I'm so upset, Mrs. McWhinny," Lily said by way of a greeting, taking tiny nibbles of a new sugar-coated model. "Jeremy just can't stop once he gets started."

"Started?"

"Taking pictures. He just goes on and on forever, and poor Whiskers, all she wants is to see her wildlife program on TV at seven, and I bet we'll never make it."

This odd conversation had the effect of propelling me back to my car — and back to my snug haven of home.

Once there, I made a cup of tea and flipped through my mail. The only portion of it that was thought provoking was trying to decide if I should buy a new turtleneck from Lands End, L. L. Bean, Norm Thompson, Orvis, or The Tog Shop, or simply drive eight miles to the Country Store in Weston.

I had nearly finished my tea when Lulu let me know in no uncertain terms that it was time I took her out for a stroll. Walking her down by the inn, I saw Jack Connors, who waved to me. At least, I think it was Connors; he was driving a car instead of his truck and seemed to be in a hurry again. Thank goodness.

When Lulu and I returned home, I reminded myself that I hadn't eaten since noon. I thought about Hilary as I poured myself a drink and put a package of frozen manicotti in the toaster oven for dinner. Good thing he wasn't here, or I'd have to listen to him read all the ingredients on the package and explain how I was heedlessly shortening my life span. This made me think, as I so often did, how incredibly lucky Hilary and I were to be leading such lively, robust lives. I'd quit smoking thirty years ago and no longer ate cheese omelets for lunch — not very big sacrifices for longevity. The only thing I can think of that my old gourmet friend had given up was mountain climbing.

I made short shrift of my meal and decided to unwind with the tube. But television didn't have much to offer, and try as I might, I couldn't get Lulu to watch the wildlife program. Giving up on being mindessly entertained, I turned off the TV and called it a night even though dusk hadn't yet fallen.

Just as I was about to start up the stairs, the phone rang and I went to answer it in Doug's den. I settled down in the old Morris chair, probably smiling because I fully expected to hear Hilary expounding on the post-dogshow doings.

It was Sophie. "Tish, oh Tish!" She was sobbing. "Hil's all right, but Bruce is dead!"

My body went cold. "Slow down, Soph. Slow down. An automobile accident, or —"

"No, Bruce was killed — murdered! — and Hilary jabbed the awl into his own leg. Tish, here's George."

"Can you hear me on this phone, Mrs. McWhinny?"

I gathered it was a portable phone and the

reception was terrible, but George's voice was firm and clear enough — which was more than I could say about myself.

George explained, "In brief, Bruce went to get something from his van — that painting — and when he didn't come back, Hilary went to find him, and soon after that Sophie went to find them both. Bruce was lying on the ground. Hilary said he turned him over, and seeing a knob protruding from his chest, pulled the thing out — an awl. I guess the shock of it made him fall to his knees, and he skewered himself."

I heard Sophie claim the telephone from George, and, calmer this time, she told me I just had to come. She'd wait for me. The police were about to arrive.

I tore my desk apart to find my night-driving glasses. They didn't make me anyone you'd want to drive with at night, but they did help. I then grabbed a flashlight, my wallet, and a thin rain cape. Lulu looked so poignant that I told her she could come, and we took off like the wind.

The broad stretch of Route 7 from Manchester to Bennington was blessedly empty and the roadsides quite visible in the deepening dusk, so I hit eighty some of the time. Ours was the first Bennington turnoff. At the fairgrounds I maneuvered around so that I could park just outside the ring of police lights.

Resting my head on the steering wheel, I counted my blessings as I took some deep breaths.

Sophie had seen me and came running over. Tight lipped and no longer weepy, she hugged me briefly, tucked my arm under hers, and we walked around the small crowd of people to the rescue squad ambulance.

All I could see were the bottoms of Hilary's big feet shod in his size twelve-and-a-half moccasins. I shuddered and suddenly recalled a sketch I'd done for someone's book jacket of a pair of large, bare feet visible at the open door of an ambulance with a nametag tied to a big toe.

"May I see him, please?" I'd stepped up the steps. "Just for a minute."

The pair in attendance didn't look too happy to see me, but the man said, "He's sort of out of it. Just say hello; we gotta move. Pronto."

Hil was as gray as the prostrate figures carved on ancient tombs and ecclesiastical coffins. I kissed the end of his mustache and brushed the hair off his forehead.

Hilary opened his eyes, saw me, and closed them. He gave my hand, which was holding his, a faint squeeze. "Bruce —"

"I know, Hil. I know."

"Bruce . . ."

"You'll have to go, lady," the attendant said.

I looked at the bottle of blood flowing into Hil's arm.

"He'll be all right?"

"Not to worry. He'll be ok."

Hilary's head rolled to one side.

"Tomorrow you can see him. I'll bet he'll be fine by then." A young female took my arm and firmly propelled me out the rear door. "We'll take good care of him, Mrs. McWhinny."

I looked at the unfamiliar, rather pretty face. "We know each other?"

"Yup. You painted me when I was ten years old. I'm Lucy Plant, remember?"

"Of course," I lied. "Yes, please, take good care of him, dear."

It was a good thing Sophie caught me or I would have fallen on my face climbing out of the ambulance.

With my index finger over my pursed lips, I gestured for Sophie to follow me.

The area surrounding Bruce's van and partially dismantled tent had been cordoned off with yellow crime scene tape. Two uniformed cops advised people to keep back. At the same time I heard one of them telling someone that no one was to leave until given express permission to do so.

Two people in casual clothes were walking around inside the cordoned area. A woman was taking pictures with the help of someone else. Either a powerful lamp blinded you or the moonless night swallowed the workers. No place is blacker than a black night in Vermont. The horizon is as high as the green mountains around you. Dusk had become night with the speed of a light switch.

Sophie nudged me and pointed to the ground a few yards on the other side of the tape. "That dark patch . . . it's so awful. I hate to tell you, but that's Hilary's blood. I thought he was dead when I first saw him." She raised a knee to show me the blood on her jeans where she must have knelt beside Hil. "From what the rescue squad said, Hil apparently jammed the awl into his inner thigh."

"An awl. George said something about an awl."

"Yeah, it was the murder weapon. Anyhow, they think Hil's hand must have forced the top of the awl down, so instead of being a puncture, it also ripped his flesh, and that's why he bled so badly. Lucy said he'd be OK?"

"He's probably in shock," George said as he came up behind us. "There he goes. Sophie says it's not far to the hospital, and those guys really know what they're doing."

"You mean guys like Lucy," Sophie said. "Where's Kim?"

"She's in her trailer. She said she wanted to be alone."

Kim had shown me her trailer just hours ago. It fit my old-fashioned idea of a trailer: a small boxy object held up by two of its own wheels and attached to the rear of her car. Inside, a cot mattress was supported by cases of dog food. Beside the bed were two huge canine futons. When I saw them, they were occupied by Donder and Blitzen, both sprawled in blissful abandon. Built-in cupboards and closets on the other wall no doubt held the rest of Kim's necessities and belongings.

Poor kid. From my brief observation last night, Kim seemed to have a happy, loving relationship with her father. Who wouldn't love Bruce?

Sophie said as much out loud.

"Maybe it was an accident," George said hopefully.

Sophie and I showed him our skeptical faces.

"An awl," George said. "I bet everybody

has an awl. I was helping some guy take down his tent a little while ago. You can tighten or loosen those guy wires with an awl. All kinds of things. Maybe Bruce was running with it and tripped on a stake or wire and killed himself."

"Sophie, you've used the word 'murder' a couple of times," I said. "Is that what the police think?"

"Well, Bruce had gone to get that painting, and where is it? Some people said it was really valuable, and it's been stolen."

"How do you know? Maybe Bruce never got back to his trailer."

I sent a fervent little prayer up to an obsidian sky: Please let this be an accident — a simple, sad accident.

"I'll need your name and address, ma'am, and your relationship to the deceased. Did you know him?" A uniformed officer with pad in hand was addressing me.

"My aunt just got here. But," Sophie added, "I've been here since noon."

As the policeman turned his attention to Sophie, I got back in the car and, hugging Lulu, watched the small bunch of people moving in and out of shadows and light.

There were some familiar shapes, but my eyes weren't good enough to identify anyone. The last thing I wanted to do was mingle with the group or make myself known to the authorities. I was thinking about poor Hilary and how he always scolded me for sticking my nose where it didn't belong. His predictable refrain was: "Let the police handle it. It's their job." Well, he'd be heartened to hear that for once I was going to obey him.

My most important activity while I waited for the interrogations to finish was sending urgent pleas to the only two saints I could think of — that is, aside from St. Francis, who I knew was busy taking care of the dogs. I called on St. Christopher and St. Jude to erase any suggestion of murder and make Bruce's demise a tragic accident.

Eleven

The next morning at 8:30 I called the Bennington hospital to inquire about Hilary. I was told he was doing well, but the informant said she didn't know if he could have visitors. In any event, visiting hours were from 11:00 to 6:00.

That gave me time for a little house cleaning, which entailed pushing around a small, airline-sized carpet sweeper and snapping a dustcloth at tabletops. Clean doesn't mean much to me; order does. I never look under rugs. I save that search for the twice-a-month treasure whom I shared with Hilary — and if Ruth could hear me call her that, she'd strangle me with her bare hands. Ruth was coming on Wednesday.

Lulu and I took a walk and ended up at the store to pick up the Sunday papers, an event that was rapidly shrinking my bank account.

As I was heading inside, Sophie, hugging a paper bag, emerged and picked her way over the usual canine barrier.

"Tish, are you going to see Hilary? Have you called yet? Is he okay?"

"All three. They say he's doing well. Can't visit till eleven. Coming?"

Sophie called our frequent disregard for personal pronouns in our conversations "goat talk." It had developed during the many times I had helped her with the funny beasts. Helped her clean the barn, lug feed, and kiss kids. She said she felt our staccato lingo was an unconscious form of bleating.

"For a million reasons I can't go now. Give Hil a big hug. This is really going to hurt him, Tish. I'm worried about him."

Her concern for Hilary almost brought tears to my eyes. I'd been trying to pretend I lived in a vacuum, and none of this had really happened. But I knew in the next hour I'd be faced with someone I loved who had a broken heart.

Sophie and I continued in our opposite directions. Newspapers in hand I walked back across to my house and got ready for my drive down to Bennington.

Before heading for the hospital I drove to Clement Hollow and parked next to Sophie's barn. Old Trixie recognized the sound of my car, or maybe she just sensed my arrival, and neighed in high C. As she greeted me effusively, I promised her an afternoon canter around the pasture one day soon or, if Sophie could join me, a trail ride through the woods.

George called and waved to me from the top of a scary-looking extension ladder that reached the eaves. "Wait for me. I want to talk to you."

Always happy to smell the fresh lumber and check the progress on Sophie's house, Lulu and I walked over to meet him. I guess I laughed out loud. Take a skinny, bare-chested, hipless fellow, add a pair of torn jeans weighted down by a carpenter's apron full of heavy tools, and you have a nearly naked man.

I suppressed the ribald comment that was on the tip of my tongue and watched him swivel around and pull up his pants.

"Excuse me. Kim says she's going to buy me a pair of overalls. What I wanted to ask you — tell you, really — was that one summer when my family rented a house on Cape Cod, I got a gofer job at the police department. The detective there took me along with him sometimes. I'm not saying I learned much but maybe a few things. Sophie says sometimes you've been able to figure things out. Well, maybe we could get together and talk."

I raised my hand. "Look, crossed fingers." I waved them in the air. "It's my hope that there's nothing to figure out. I hope that Bruce's death is a terrible mistake."

"You mean, he fell on the awl he was carrying?" He shook his head. "From where I sit, it's no accident. The cops couldn't find the painting last night. At least they were still looking when we left. You can bet someone's got it. Kim's down in Bennington now. We'll know more soon."

"How's she taking it?"

"She cried herself to sleep last night, but she went off this morning in fighting trim. You know more about paintings than I do. What about it? Do you think it's really valuable?"

"Maybe to someone." I shrugged. "I wouldn't know. Perhaps there'll be something among Bruce's papers that will tell us about the painting's provenance — you know, background." I recrossed my fingers and murmured, "Heaven forbid, George. Forget what Sophie said about my sleuthing. I have trouble finding my glasses a dozen times a day."

We chatted a moment or two longer, and then Lulu and I got into my car and headed south. Every one of the five miles between Lofton and Bennington made me feel increasingly grim. I had a miserable premonition that the saints had let me down.

Reaching Bennington, I found the hospital in short order and made it to the correct floor with no trouble. But a firm young woman at the nurses' station told me I'd have to wait until someone did something or other before I could see Hilary.

As I prepared to make my case, the nurse said, "Here they are."

Two men were walking toward us. Mutt was a small bandy-legged middle-aged man. Jeff, on his left, was a tall, narrow young fellow wearing huge aviator glasses.

"This lady wants to visit the patient in seventeen."

I introduced myself. They had to shake my outstretched hand and tell me that Mutt was Detective Apple and Jeff was Sergeant Dever.

"I'm a close friend of Hilary Oats's and eager to see him. How is he?"

"He's okay." Detective Apple looked around and led us to empty chairs in a corner. "Can we talk a minute please, Mrs. . . ."

"McWhinny. I'm a neighbor of Mr. Oats in Lofton. I didn't arrive at the fairgrounds last night until eight, just after you all did. I came in response to a call from Sophie

Beaumont, my niece, who found Bruce Hemphill and his godfather."

I started to rise. I hoped my statement had covered enough ground so that I could go see Hilary.

Detective Apple waved me back down with his pad. "Please. A few questions. Did the deceased know that his godfather had left his house and property in Lofton to Miss Beaumont?"

I couldn't have been more surprised. "What? Who told you that?"

"Please answer the question."

"I have no idea, and I can't imagine why it would matter. Ask Hilary Oats. Have you found the painting?"

"We will. Are you of the opinion that Mr. Oats was angry at the deceased because being of an improvident nature he had nonetheless bought a valuable painting?"

"Of course not. You don't understand. Hilary adored Bruce; he doted on him. Surely you must have seen he's heartbroken. This is preposterous."

Neither of them seemed to like their thoughts thusly characterized. I took a deep breath and told myself to cool down. But I couldn't stop. "I'm not sure 'improvident' is an accurate description of Bruce. Who told you that?"

"We haven't been idle." Sergeant Dever came close to a snarl. "You, we learned, are an artist. What value would you put on" — he checked his pad — "the picture, the painting of two dogs?"

"I'm not the one to ask. You might try the curators at the Bennington Museum." They weren't crazy about being advised, either. I stood up. "Please, I want to see Mr. Oats."

Detective Apple gave a faint smile. "We can see what team you're on."

"Team? What team? I'm on the team that wants to catch the person who killed harmless, lovable Bruce Hemphill. And I certainly hope that's you two gentlemen."

They managed twin shrugs and assured me we'd be seeing each other.

Before I reached room seventeen, Sergeant Dever called, "Mrs. McWhinny, we'd like you to look over the list we left with Mr. Oats. See if there are any names you can add."

I nodded and continued on. Hilary's door opened as a nurse made her exit. I shouldn't have called it "Hilary's door." He shared the room with two other patients. Thanks to partially drawn curtains, I could only see feet and their TV sets flickering overhead.

Hilary's face might have been a death mask. I'd made quite a few such masks of the living. Your willing model slathers his or her face and hair with Vaseline and with a straw sticking out of each nostril is packed in wet plaster of paris. When the hardened mold is removed, it's filled with fresh plaster.

That's how Hilary looked: as white as plaster and as still as death. He opened tear-filled eyes at my approach.

Hilary and I hugged each other for a while. Then he poked me and pointed. "Better get that chair before someone else grabs it."

I did, pulling it close to the bed, and leaned on the bed guard. "You feel like talking?"

"Sure, for what it's worth."

"What happened?"

"It was a pretty jolly crowd, and everyone had a thermos of something to drink, like a cocktail party. Bruce was a little the worse for wear but happy. He allowed as how he wanted everyone to get a better look at his awesome painting." Hilary managed the faintest of smiles when he intoned the popular adjective for the critters.

"He went off to get it, and after a while we began to wonder where he was. I said I'd go find him. There just behind his tent I found him, lying facedown on the grass. I figured

Bruce was a little tight and had probably tripped over one of those guy wires. I grabbed his shoulder and turned him over." Hilary looked away.

"I've seen a lot of dead men, Tish." He turned back, his eyes brimming with tears. "I knew, I knew . . . I saw a handle sticking out of his chest, and I guess I thought there might be a spark of life if I pulled it out. When I saw the bloody thing in my hands, I guess I fell on my knees and stuck the damn thing in my leg." He touched his left leg. "Sophie said I was just sitting there bleeding. Guess it was shock."

"I thought you were in shock when I saw you in the ambulance last night."

Hilary raised his eyebrows. "You saw me last night?" He covered his eyes with a hand. "Who would do a thing like that, Tish? Who would hurt someone like . . ." He turned away again. "But I know why. That painting. Bruce's death is as much my fault as though I'd killed him with my own hands. How, why, did I ever get you to paint on that damn picture? I hope Alice can't look down on the shameful mess I've made."

"Don't talk that way, Hil. Fault, what does that matter now? And you didn't 'get me' to patch up that painting. I'm quite responsible for my own actions. I do agree with you, though. Bruce wasn't killed by a murderer, he was killed by a thief who wanted the painting."

"Anyway, the police were just here asking me a million questions."

"I saw them," I said. "They asked me some questions, too."

"Then you know what I know. They think I might have killed him. It was my awl — at least I think it was. When Bruce was at the house the other day, I found a carpenter's awl in the barn — you know, the one I used to use to make holes in belts and stuff. Thinking he could probably use it, I tossed it in his van." Hilary put his hands over his face. "I'm going to be sick."

I quickly handed him a towel from the bedstand and pressed the buzzer hanging from equipment behind him. Hil was struggling to sit up, and I wasn't much help, but from a lower shelf I took one of those hospital spittoons and put it in his hand. After a bit I realized Hilary wasn't retching; he was sobbing.

A nurse brushed me aside, and, exuding confidence and efficiency, she leaned over Hilary's shaking form. I mumbled something about giving Hil some privacy and left the room.

Once out in the hallway, I leaned back

against the wall and closed my eyes. My head might as well have been in a black cloud because that's all my mind's eye could see. Poor Hilary, blaming himself for the killing of the apple of his eye. Sophie's expression "over the hill" came to me. I hoped this tragedy wouldn't push Hilary over the hill and out of reach.

Ten minutes later the nurse emerged with an armload of laundry and a slop pail. She smiled as though nothing had happened and said that Hilary was just fine and wanted to see me.

Never underestimate an old warrior. I thanked her and went back inside.

Hilary didn't look fine, but he was sitting up in bed looking tidy and was clearly in control of himself. He pointed at a sheet of paper on the back of the bedside table.

"Ah," I said. "This is the list the police were talking about. People known to be present in the group at the time of the incident — approximately 7:00 P.M. to 8:30 P.M. I'll read the list. Stop me if I come to a name you know." I picked up a pencil.

"We'll probably do better if I tell you who wasn't there." Then he said no to a dozen names.

"The Blounts," he said, "were there. Jeremy at least, but I didn't see Lily. What good is this list? They must have compiled it from asking everyone who was there. Of course, I know about the Loftonites — who was there, who wasn't. But there must have been others milling around who thought they could steal the painting. Lots of people might have thought it was a cinch, you know, to steal from easygoing Bruce; and as I said, he'd been knocking back the drinks. Anybody could have done it." Hilary brightened for a moment. "If I did it, where's the painting?"

"Good point. They can't possibly think you had anything to do with it, anyhow. They're just trying to stir things up. See if they can learn anything. Put it out of your mind, Hil."

Put it out of your mind. What a stupid thing to say. It wasn't his mind or the thought of blame that worried me. It was the terrible image of Bruce lying dead that I knew Hilary could never escape.

The nurse stood in the doorway. "The doctor's coming. Maybe you can step outside."

I patted the telephone on the table. "I'll call you later." I blew Hil a kiss and left.

Twelve

Reflecting on my brief abrasive chat with the law, I realized I could no longer fool myself. Bruce had been murdered because someone wanted the painting. Those damn critters. How could I have ever been so stupid, as to be a part — the biggest part — of Bruce's hoax? Or was I? I didn't plan on any heavy self-flagellation, but I wanted to rethink dear, sweet Bruce's role. If the painting hadn't had Landseer's signature, would this have happened? I was convinced that the answer was no, absolutely not.

But what to do now? How could I unravel the mystery and keep my skirts clean? I recalled what I'd told Hilary — that the detectives just wanted to stir things up — and it gave me an idea. Probably a lousy idea but worth a try.

I picked up the phone, and after some discussion with the operator I got the Connorses' phone number. Luckily my call was answered by Jean. Luckily, because I was in no mood for Jack's jocular banter.

I think I liked Jean; I wasn't quite sure. She was friendly on the telephone and told me what I wanted to know.

"Yes, the dog show is tomorrow, Monday, at Craftsbury Common. Wherever that is. I haven't looked at the map yet."

"You'll love it, Jean." I tried inadequately to describe that inviting town that sat on a high plateau in the Northeast Kingdom. "Are you going to show?"

"I hope so, though I haven't much heart for it," Jean said. "The dogs seem well, and I'd like to go up with Kim. I don't know if she'll go. It's been a terrible time for her, but it might be a good idea to get away. I have to admit I'm no real help to her. We've never been able to talk to each other, except, of course, about dogs. We'll see. I did persuade her to let me make the funeral arrangements. We decided on a simple graveside good-bye in Concord two weeks from now."

"What a ghastly scene it was. Were you both there last night when it happened?"

"Kim and I were. Jack said he wasn't there, that he'd gone home. But you'd have to ask him. About the show tomorrow, it's quite informal. It's a match show."

"Match?" I'd never heard the term.

"Yes. Match shows are popular with most fanciers, and there's not a lot of stiff competition. It's a good time to try out dogs and handlers, too. The other kind of show, point shows, like yesterday, are run by the American Kennel Club. When your dog wins, he gets points toward his championship."

I told Jean I might go, and if I did, I hoped we could find some time together.

I hung up and immediately picked up the phone again to call Sophie. Usually it was easier to talk to Sophie if you went to Goat Heaven instead of calling her on the telephone, but I had no desire to be clubby with George, nice as he was.

Sophie answered the phone on the first ring.

"I'm on a rafter, Tish! Guess what? I got a cellular phone. It's magic and so small, I can put it in my pocket."

I almost said "Capital idea," but remembered that the last time I used the words, she told me I sounded like a real period piece. (She'd been even more aghast one day when she caught me jiggling my own phone and asking for central.)

"The first person I called on this fabulous new tool, Tish, was Hilary at the hospital. He tried to sound cheerful, but he didn't fool me. I'll go see him later. Tomorrow I'm going to a goat show in Hardwick. Wanna come?"

That was exactly what I wanted to do because I hoped to give birth to my new idea in Craftsbury Common. I could drop Sophie off in Hardwick, proceed to the dog show, and pick her up on the way home. Or, if Hilary was in good shape and I felt he didn't need us, we could spend the night at the heavenly Inn on the Common. Aside from good food, they've earned three stars from me because they have the grace to welcome dogs.

During the rest of the day I puttered around. I talked to Hilary a few times. Once I woke him up.

"Awake or asleep, Tish, it doesn't matter to me. Maybe it's time for the big sleep."

To hear Hilary say that was like having some giant hand squeeze my heart.

It wasn't possible to come up with appropriate pep talk at a time like this, but for the moment one wasn't required.

Sophie's voice came on the line as she apparently grabbed the phone away from Hilary. "Just came in, Tish. Don't worry about this old chieftain. I've brought him an airline-sized bottle of scotch and some yummy lobster meat. We're going to feast."

I didn't have time to count all my blessings, so I quit after the first one: Sophie.

When we hung up, I returned to the mundane matters at hand. My marketing list was uninteresting, but I couldn't put it off and decided to erase my errands before heading for the Northeast Kingdom. I hadn't looked at a map lately, but I knew it must be at least a three-hour drive.

I drove to Londonderry and parked in front of the hairdresser's. I could see that Phyllis, our perky manicurist, was at liberty when I walked in.

"There you are." She jumped to her feet. "I know you want to look like a lady again." Our little joke.

While my deft friend practiced her art, she discoursed on the infinite variety of matter found under clients' fingernails. "Paint is number one, and you're the winner there, Mrs. McWhinny. Though one of your friends came close just a while ago."

"Really? Who's that?"

"Mrs. Conner, I believe she said her name was. She was here with Millie Santini one day." Phyllis continued with her review. "Next after paint comes ink, I mean globs of it. You should see Albert's fingernails." Albert produced our local newspaper. "I won't even mention auto mechanics. I turn them away. I had a tough case Saturday of Elmer's glue."

I made an effort to digest these facts even though I felt I couldn't dine out on this particular lot of esoteric knowledge.

After my beauty touch-up, I headed to the hardware store. I was so busy admiring my nails that I almost missed the duet I caught a glimpse of through the window at the Idlenot Restaurant. I stopped and inched back a few steps until I was partially hidden behind the wall phone box and took a careful look at the pair.

Ian Bixler, no longer dressed for center ring, looked very snappy in a rugby shirt. He was massaging the back of Jean Connors's neck. Fondling was a better word. Ian's head was bent in front of hers as though he was uttering a last tender word before a kiss.

My absorption with the scene in the booth was total. In fact, I was so transported that I had moved out from behind the telephone box and almost had my nose pressed against the window.

I was brought to my senses by Ian, who was waving both hands over his head. In fact, they were both waving me in as though they could hardly wait for me to join their smooching party.

Who was this woman Jean? I would have guessed she had a better chance of being a cold fish than a woman of towering passion.

Not that playing a little footsie in front of God and all of Londonderry indicated unbridled passion.

And what about Jack? Where did he fit in? I had a wild vision of a lassoed Ian, being pulled along a dirt road behind Jack's truck.

Reluctant to intrude, I pretended not to comprehend their gestures and put on a charade of shading my eyes with my hand, looking puzzled, as I backed away toward the grocery store.

No luck. Ian rushed out of the restaurant babbling jolly inanities, dragged me back inside, and propelled me onto the bench of the booth.

"Here you are, Tish," said the young waitress, whom I probably knew as a child. "See, iced tea for you, just the way you like it."

Jean and Ian seemed relaxed and happy, but I felt awkward.

"Are you going to be judging at the show tomorrow, Ian?" I asked, flailing for conversation.

"Not tomorrow. It's my day to canvass some of the antiques stores in Manchester and Dorset. I'm looking for" — his eyes lost their twinkle — "you know, dog paintings. But it's hard to think of anything but this terrible tragedy. I only met Bruce once or twice, and he was such a fine chap; I'm sure his death had nothing to do with his character but was caused by that painting."

"Greed," Jean said. "When you think of the enormous competitive air at a dog show. The rivalries, the envy, and then altogether too many less than honorable owners and handlers, it's remarkable that no one has ever been killed before this."

"What a description!" I said, thinking of my one experience as an exhibitor when I was a child. "I think of dog lovers as the nicest possible people!"

"Most of them are, Tish. But we have our share of cheats and stinkers. Think of all those miserable puppy mills. I can promise you they're not run by dog lovers. Or the really evil breeders who pounce on the popularity of some breed and thoughtlessly inbreed, only to produce heartbreaking mutants."

"Stop! I don't want to hear any more."

Ian asked me what I thought of the painting — "As an artist, Tish."

I denied having an opinion but said that if it was a real Landseer, it might be just the kind of painting his client had wanted.

Jean smiled and patted some part of Ian's anatomy under the table. "He's so secretive about his client — aren't you?"

When Ian then patted Jean's hand, I

began to think that all this patting and rubbing must be the influence of the dog world. They treated each other like dogs, and I wondered if on more private occasions they scratched each other's ears.

Curiosity overcame my desire to escape, and I asked how long the chummy couple had known each other.

They beamed at the question. "Since last year," Ian said. "It was Labor Day in Providence."

"At McDonald's," Jean simpered.

How could this chilly-voiced, dun-colored woman turn into a kitten? And although Ian had lost none of his charm, his sappy display of affection for Jean had definitely reduced his attraction for me. If I were in his shoes, I think I'd be kind of afraid of Jack, who seemed to like flexing his muscles and be perceived as the well-heeled, self-made rugged Texan. And what's more, I'd heard there was still a law on the books in Texas that permitted a man to shoot an unfaithful wife.

I'd had enough. I looked at my watch. "Oh, my Lord. I've got to go. I'm expecting someone at home, and I really should be there." Without giving them time to protest, I jumped up and hurried out of the restaurant.

I had plenty of time during my drive home to ponder this latest turn of events.

I hadn't been home long before the phone rang. It was Ian, who said he was sorry we hadn't had a chance to talk at all, and would I consider a light supper at the Lofton Inn with him? Now. Tonight.

It took me so long to decide that Ian had to ask, "Are you still on the line?"

I don't like snoopy people. I hated to think I was one of them, but I tried without luck to think of a gentler word to describe the reason I accepted Ian's invitation. The Idlenot meeting had left me with little desire to see the old smoocher, but I thought it might be a good idea to find out more about his pilgrimage on his client's behalf. Was Ian specifically trying to find a painting of two terriers hunting?

I said yes and headed back out the door.

It's always a pleasure to eat at the Lofton Inn. The old pine walls and great stone fireplace are real, and the low beams aren't made of painted styrofoam glued to the ceiling but were hand-hewn by someone's great-grandfather. Candles flicker in trios from wall sconces made by the local blacksmith. The bar has been stained by years of spilled grog and its surface polished by an army of elbows.

Sitting on a barstool, Ian looked rosy-cheeked and full of good cheer. He also looked much better to me without Jean beside him. He slipped off his barstool and kissed my hand with unobtrusive elegance.

"Why," he asked, "does a gentleman kiss a lady's hand?"

I asked the requisite "Why?"

"A fellow's got to start somewhere."

It was the first time I'd laughed in twenty-four hours. It felt good.

We made our way to a table in the dining room where, at Ian's urging, I sketched in my life and career during the last four decades. When it was Ian's turn, he told me his wife had been a semi-invalid for years and stayed at their cottage on Gibraltar while he spent most of his time at his flat in London.

"We tolerate old sailors at home, and they still have me sitting on the Waterways Commission. Keeps me out of trouble — at least some of the time. My love is poking around antiques shops and flea markets, looking for that rare find."

After a dinner of trout, green salad, and a bottle of Vermont chardonnay, we sat by the fire warming handsome snifters of brandy (which I knew I'd regret). Our easy chatter ended when Ian said he felt sorry for Hilary.

"Oh, I do, too. I know he'll grieve over Bruce, but physically he'll be fine. He's a tough old bird."

"I don't doubt that, Tish. I meant he'll be in a position of having quite a lot of explaining to do."

My eyebrows rose.

"Jean tells me that Bruce was almost constantly in Oats's debt, and it could be argued that for some special reason his patience was brought to the breaking point. Perhaps Bruce demanded too much just once too often. So Oats kills Bruce, maybe — in fact, probably — by mistake. You know, grabbed his arm or something and Bruce falls. He's horrified, then tries and fails to take his own life." He paused somewhat dramatically then added, "And don't forget the awl belonged to Oats."

"How do you know that?"

"I heard that Oats told the cops himself. He apparently put the awl in Bruce's van when he spent the night there. Doesn't look good."

"You seem to have dismissed the painting." I was incensed. "Where is it?"

"I wish I knew. I can tell you it wasn't dismissed by anyone after the show, even though the police at the time seemed to think it was an accident. Everyone was talking about the painting. Anyone could have stolen it. Who knows? I'm going to be seeing a lot of dealers tomorrow. Maybe I can smoke out some information. You know, I'd love to have that painting for my client, so I don't have to pretend sincerity in my inquiries."

"What makes you think anyone's going to tell you anything that they know about the painting? It's stolen property, for Pete's sake."

"I can be persuasive," Ian said with a leer. "We'll solve this, Tish. I find the painting, I buy it, my client will be ecstatic, and you'll have the murderer."

"I don't want the murderer, and I don't give a damn about the painting. I want the police to find the murderer, and if they find the painting, fine." That wasn't quite true, but I was sort of annoyed with Ian's blithe scenario. "This client of yours, Ian — I get the feeling there's some considerable clout there. How persuasive can you be about getting whatever it is you're looking for?"

"Persuasive?" Ian flushed. "You aren't implying, are you, Letitia, that I would exert improper force on anyone?"

I squeezed his hand. "Of course not, Ian, of course not."

But what did I really know about Ian aside

from our brief wartime love affair? I'd never seen him on his own turf, in his own home, or with his family or friends. I could almost hear Sophie telling me to cool it, butt out, don't look for trouble. Easier said than done.

Emboldened by my mulled mind, I asked Ian if his enthusiasm for Jean Connors had been blessed by Jack.

The fire made Ian's cheeks look even pinker as he reflected on my question.

"From the moment I met Jean last year, she struck me as a cry for help. I suppose I took her icy exterior as a sort of a challenge, too. The woman needed a little attention, some affection. I think Jack's a big bluff. In a daily way he pops in and out of her life. God knows what he does the rest of the time. You know, Tish, if Jean told me their relationship was platonic, I'd believe her. Jack's probably happy. He likes having a cool WASP at his side."

"Are you saying he condones your attentions to Jean?"

"Hardly that. He and I have only met occasionally and briefly at dog shows. Jean never talks about Jack. I think she loves him. And disabuse yourself of the idea that we're conducting a torrid affair. It's more like snuggling. She needs a friend, and it makes me happy to make her happy."

"Bravo."

Ian and I walked back to my house, where Lulu joined us for a stroll from one end of the village to the other.

"This is my last year on the dog show circuit," he said. "It's been fun, but I'm sick of it."

"Tired of dogs?"

"Lord, no. I'm tired of dog people. Owners; handlers, breeders. Now Lulu, here" — he picked her up — "that's the kind of dog for me. She doesn't have to show off her figure or make us admire her skill or her spirit. All she has to do is love us."

With that, Ian and Lulu did some heavy snuggling of their own. We said good night, and I watched his jaunty figure dissappear at the bend in the road heading toward the inn.

Thirteen

Before going to bed, I called Hilary, who said the doctor wanted him to stay in the hospital for one more day. He encouraged Sophie and me to go to Craftsbury and assured me he'd be fine. I did not confide my scheme to stir things up — to him or to Sophie.

Sophie, Lulu, and I took off for our trip at dawn and made our first pit stop at Hanover at seven o'clock. We found a cozy spot with sinfully good croissants and spine-straightening coffee.

Then Sophie took her turn at the wheel, and we were back on the highway. Sometimes I preferred her divided attention to her undivided attention. Maybe I could pry some information out of her.

I pulled out my favorite writing equipment — a felt point pen and an assortment of cards. My daily mail caters to my taste. I love the feeling of my pen moving along on rich vellum. I use the backs of invitations — a benefit evening at two hundred a head or a wedding invitation, which always has an extravagant amount of unused space.

"You going to write something?"

"That's my intention, but you have to talk to me. Answer questions. Now. Please. You must have seen Kim last night. What, if anything, did she find out from the detectives?"

"Maybe they're not telling her what they know, but all she said was that they had no clues. She asked if they'd found any fingerprints on the awl, and they just said these things take time. Footprints, ditto. And you know, Tish, it's been dry; the ground's hard as rock. They said, yes, there were prints in and all over her father's van. But, as Kim said, that was no news. Dozens of friends went in and out of it all the time. It was his home."

"What's Kim like? Other than dinner the other night, I only caught a glimpse of her Saturday. Tell me."

"Well, she's a great skier."

I drew a range of mountains at the top of the card.

"She loves animals."

I drew Lulu inside a heart. I asked about Kim's relationship to George. "Have she and George been involved for a long time?"

"I don't know how long they've been involved." She emphasized the word "involved" with sarcasm, as though it was another of my quaint words.

"What's it to you, Tish? How would I know?"

I said I thought George was a very attractive young man, and wished I didn't sound so much like Hilary.

"Well, bully for you." She passed a wobbling double truck and showed the driver her middle finger.

"Come on, help me, Soph. I want to think about poor Bruce and what might have happened and all the whys and wherefores. Was Kim fond of her mother and father?"

"As far as I know. She was at college when they were divorced, and she's always had summer jobs. I don't suppose she saw much of either of them. Then she married that jerk what's-his-name, and they had twenty cows on a farm in the middle of Maine. I couldn't stand him, but I visited them once." She chuckled. "Kim does everything all the way, and she was really into cows — and I mean into. I found her in the barn once with her arm up to her elbow in a cow's behind. And, oh, God, she kept semen in jars in the refrigerator. I mean, you just don't forage around for your lunch in her house."

I digested that alarming information and

asked Sophie if Kim liked her stepfather.

"I guess she thinks he's a harmless blowhard but nice and rich. But, Tish, I've hardly talked to her. When would I?"

"That night after the dog show. But never mind. Did you see Jeremy or Lily after the show?"

"Saw him. And speaking of Kim, Jeremy was all over her like a blanket. Made me feel sorry for Lolita, but I didn't see her."

"Wasn't George with Kim?"

"Not really."

That was all Sophie would say. I wrote "no" on the eggshell vellum and put my cards away.

We discussed our plans for the day and decided to stick together. Sophie said she wanted to see the cashmere bucks and talk to a couple of breeders. She thought the whole visit shouldn't take more than half an hour. I hoped my visit to Craftsbury Common would be equally brief.

The array of vehicles at the goat show featured lots of covered pickups, farm trucks, and plain old cars. I didn't see any grand RVs like Jean Connors's. One perky nanny watched me from the window of an old Lincoln Town Car.

As much as I wanted to greet each and every goat in the big tent, I resisted. I knew

Lulu would be unwelcome, and it was too hot to leave her in the car, so we strolled around until Sophie returned bearing three beautiful long hot dogs, one for each of us. After our fine lunch, I drove the few miles to Craftsbury Common.

The little gathering on the broad lawn looked like the second coming or perhaps a ring of covered wagons protecting the pioneers. But before we joined the group, I had to introduce Sophie to the town's treasure. The small library was closed for the day, but through a side window we could admire the famous painting of Colonel Crafts and his son.

The colonel had cleared twelve acres of land, where in 1788 he built a sawmill and a gristmill. Forty years later he became the governor of the state, and that may have been when this stunning portrait was painted. It was remarkable that it hadn't been claimed by a museum. Sophie was suitably impressed, but we had, after all, come for the dog show, and we made our way back to the crowd.

We then checked our watches. My errand was private, so we separated and agreed to meet at the car in an hour. We had both been thinking about Hilary and decided to skip fine food and drink and a luxurious night at the inn and just head for home by noon.

An informal show would surely not turn away Lulu, so we marched into the milling group like a couple of champions, and I made my way to Phil Tune's display of dog-adorned art. It was half the size of the one in Bennington, but it was still a remarkable array of his works.

Even though we hadn't met in Bennington, I knew it was Phil who greeted me. Tune was a scruffy, small man in one-size-fits-all woodsman clothes. He wore his black cap pulled so far down, he had to tilt his head back to see me. It was a good thing he met his public out-of-doors because he was that rare sight: a chain-smoker of the type who never removed the cigarette from his mouth. His wispy mustache appeared to be smoking, too.

I guess I studied him longer than was polite because he managed a smile and said, "I don't inhale." What a joke. How could he help it?

We shook hands, and he allowed as how I looked familiar.

Then I propositioned him. I handed him a Polaroid of the repaired painting of the critters. "What will you charge me to do a quick copy of this? I know you've seen the original."

Tune chuckled as though I'd handed him the funny papers. There certainly wasn't anything funny about the picture — so considering it a nervous tic, I said nothing.

"Don't know what you're up to, lady. I'll do it for you, but no antiquing the canvas or no signature, no stuff like that."

"Good. How much?"

"Well, I paint people's dogs a lot, and it depends on the size. And this is a straight, direct painting, right? No underpainting or glazes, nothing like that, right?"

"Right. It's eighteen by twenty."

"For a quick job, say two hundred dollars."

"Great. Where do you live, Phil?"

"Bellows Falls."

"Great. Tell me, did you know Bruce Hemphill at all well?"

He shook his head as he lit another cigarette. "Not well. I just moved east from around Chicago. We talked some these last few shows. Nice guy. Makes me sick to think what happened to him, nice guy like that."

"I wish someone would tell me what you do with a painting you've stolen," I said. "Who would buy it? Who could sell it? Seems crazy."

I gave Tune two fifty-dollar bills and promised him the rest when it was delivered.

"How quick is quick? Say, Thursday?"

"Sure. I'll put this picture in my enlarger, draw it on the canvas, and block the whole thing in. Needs one day to dry, then another day to finish it up. At least that's how I do it if all goes well. But this is a pretty good picture, and, like you say, I've seen the original, so it shouldn't be too tough."

We both smiled hard and shook hands, and Tune promised to call me Thursday.

I walked around the show ring trying to find Jean Connors and came upon her leaning against Jack's car, eating an ice cream cone. It looked awfully good.

"Jean, stay there." I backtracked, returning in a few minutes with my own double-dip of pistachio in a crisp sugar cone. "Where's your palace on wheels?"

"My palace" — Jean laughed — "is also our guest room. Jack has some business friend spending the night. Besides, this is easier." She patted the car. "And the dogs love it. More windows."

"Jack's business?" I asked. "I guess I don't know exactly what his field is."

"You name it, Jack's in it. Real estate, oil, syndicates for heaven-knows-what. All he needs is a telephone and wheels. Makes life nice for me. I don't have to adjust to his life; he's happy anyplace."

Aren't you lucky, I thought. All this and Ian, too. Behind Jean's head I saw a red ribbon hung on the half-open car window. "A prize! Who won it?"

"Macho, here, brought it to me." She hugged the handsome winner. "He's disgusted; he expected a blue."

"This business must be awfully hard on the dogs. Although your pooches seem happy."

"Hard on them!" She kissed Macho. "You've got it back to front, Tish. We fanciers feel sorry for dogs like, well, like your sweet Lulu. Why, they're bored to tears. Lulu has no challenges. All she has to do is make you happy and obey the house rules. Show dogs work and like to strut their stuff." She pointed to a small group of mixed breeds trotting around the ring. "Look at them. They love it. Can you see that red chow being shown by that young girl? He'll get the blue."

"Oh, dear," I said. "Is the show rigged?"

"No, ma'am, but take a look at the judge."

There was nothing unusual that I could see about the pudgy, carrot-topped woman who was obviously the judge.

"It happens again and again, you'll see. The prize goes to the dog that most resembles the judge."

"How about Queen Bea? Do you show her at these informal shows?"

"No. She loves showtime, but it might be too stressful. No rulings have been put out yet by the Kennel Club, but I suspect a dog with a pacemaker wouldn't be acceptable."

"A pacemaker! That's a new one. Not to be crass, but that must cost a million dollars!"

"Almost, but it's not as bad as buying a new one. They can cost as much as eight or ten thousand dollars."

My puzzled expression led Jean to elaborate. "For dogs, they implant used ones. They take pacemakers from people who have died. Most of them have years of life to go. They're small, you know, just a wire and a battery the size of a bar of hotel soap — you'd never know Queenie had one unless I showed you."

"I can imagine it now. What a delicious racket. Your friendly funeral director, unbeknownst to the loved ones left behind, removes his dead client's gizmo and sells it to your vet for a hefty price."

I guess Hilary is right; I *do* have a devious mind.

Jean had more news of implants. It seems the queen of England had microchips the size of a grain of rice implanted under the skin of some of her corgies so that they can be traced if they're lost or stolen.

We both stepped back to let a brace of Dobermans charge by. Jean was outraged at the sight of a small blond toddler leading the largest of all dogs, an Irish wolfhound.

"A sight like that," she said, "drives me wild. If that behemoth was startled or suddenly attracted to another dog, with one leap it could mash that child against a tree or Lord knows what. Why, last week I saw an Amstaff—"

"A what?"

"An American Staffordshire terrier. It grabbed an untended Yorkie and in one shake broke its neck — probably thought it was a rat — and —"

"Enough." I tightened my hold on Lulu. "You're scaring me to death."

Still frowning, Jean, with Macho and Missy, wove her way toward the center ring.

I moved along, still licking my cone and basking in the country scene: the dogs, the people, the background.

"When I described some dog owners," Jean said, "did I tell you some of them were incredibly stupid? Whoops, sorry. Someone I have to speak to." She abruptly wove her way toward the center ring.

"Look out!" the warning came inches

from my ear as someone grabbed my arm.

The car surging toward us looked like the final curtain to me. Adrenaline made me leap backward, nearly decapitating Lulu at the end of her leash and throwing us both against the radiator of a truck. I slid off the bumper to my knees and watched as the killer car momentarily stopped just short of a baby carriage. It was then I realized it was the Connorses' car. Oh, Lord! Jean's mother cocker, Queen Bea, could she be in the car? As I was struggling to my feet, Jean raced by me yelling, "Stop! Help! Stop that car!"

I caught up with her as she almost touched the car's trunk. Suddenly it swerved sideways and spurted across the common as everyone watched it bump onto the road and disappear from sight.

Jean asked if I'd seen the driver.

All I had seen was a dark cap on a genderless head.

Jean seemed about to crumble as two of us reached for her arms. Her other supporter was a solid-looking man.

"Your car?" he asked.

Jean nodded.

I said, "Yes."

"Did you leave the keys in it?" The man spoke with calm authority, and it seemed to bring Jean out of her stunned condition.

"No." She held out her hand to display a ring of keys.

"I'm Ratner. Sheriff Joe Ratner." He unhitched a phone from his belt and relayed information into it as he quizzed Jean.

"Kind of car? Jaguar. Color blue. License number?"

Jean looked it up in her wallet.

"Anything of value in the car? No."

"Queen Bea?" I asked.

"No, thank the Lord. She's home."

With that assurance I relaxed and realized I was in considerable pain. Intending to sit on a nearby camp chair, I tripped over a dog, missed the chair, and landed hard on my bottom. It hurt so, I burst into tears and hid my face on Lulu, who had sympathetically nestled on my lap. Tearfully, I dissuaded a kind soul who was trying to pull me to my feet. "Please don't."

Then, thank goodness, Sophie was kneeling beside me. "Good God, what's this?" She was looking in disgust at the pale-green mess of ice cream smeared over my chest. Fending off helpers, she gradually got me upright.

"Anything broken?"

"My spirit."

"Shall we get you to a doctor?"

I shook my head in response to all her

other questions until she asked if I wanted to go get in the car. I did. After tucking me into the Isuzu, Sophie left for a few minutes returning with a container of tea and magically producing two aspirin.

I was no help to the sheriff, who leaned on the car door to ask me to describe the scene and the driver.

Those damn baseball caps, everybody wears them. Unless a distinctive mark or message is advertised on the front, they are hopeless for identification. And I'm sure no one has ever picked a suspect out of a police lineup by the back of his or her head.

"Hair?" the sheriff asked.

"If there had been anything unusual about its hair, I'd have noticed. What did Mrs. Connors say?"

"She's no help, either."

Sophie stuck her head through the other window. "We're driving Jean home — OK, Tish?"

"Of course, but please let's get going. I'm going to expire."

Sophie said a state trooper had just arrived, and Jean had to fill out a report. The trooper promised it wouldn't take long.

I have serious trouble with dawdlers. Thank goodness the trooper was quick and efficient, and twenty minutes later we were headed south with Jean and her two cockers in back. Lulu was curled up between Sophie and me on the front seat.

Jean thanked us profusely and kept repeating that she couldn't believe it. That here in this sweet little town someone was so vile as to steal Jack's car. She said she was overcome with a headache of terrible intensity and had just taken knockout pills.

I wished that I had some myself but was grateful when Jean lapsed into drugged silence, obviating the need for conversation.

I managed to scrunch down in my seat and slipped between nausea, sleep, and dark thoughts while Sophie drove my boxy wagon as though it was a ground-hugging sports car. The only sound was Lulu's snoring and Sophie's unprintable comments to other, less skillful drivers with whom she was forced to share the road.

Jean surfaced a few times on the ride home. We aired the dogs, ate some junk, and shared a couple of cokes. With unspoken consent, we barely mentioned the horrid event. In fact, we hardly spoke to each other at all. Thanks to Sophie's fine driving and the music on public radio, the trip was mercifully swift.

We weren't expected home until much later, so I didn't even call Hilary when we arrived. Instead, I used a half a box of Epsom salts in the bathtub and stayed in so long, I could have used a forklift to get me out. Then I hit my bed, ate a couple of Fig Newtons, took a quick look at the newspaper, and passed out.

Fourteen

I'd been sleeping for eight hours when the telephone wakened me. It was Hilary. I said we'd had an adventure, which I would tell him about on our drive home from the hospital. I promised to be there promptly at ten o'clock.

The next call was from a very somber Jack Connors. He wanted me to describe every second of yesterday's dramatic episode. He kept pressing me for a description of the thief, which, of course, was hopeless. He said Jean was miserable, and he was going to insist that she stay in bed for the day. I wondered how well "insist" played in their family.

Sophie called to see if I felt better. I did, but older. No special part of my anatomy had suffered injury. It was my entire armature that had been jolted.

I asked her to tell George that if he wanted to play detective, why didn't he try to figure out who stole the Connorses' car and why.

"I know why," she said. "The same reason anyone steals anything: money. I don't know what Jags cost — maybe fifty grand."

It seemed inconceivable to me that anyone would spend that amount of money on a car. I often thought of Hilary's shibboleth: Two things you can't tell anybody — who to love and how to spend money.

At the appointed hour, I drove down to Bennington to retrieve the philosopher himself from the hospital and take him home. Hilary looked very uncomfortable beside me in the car but insisted that he was just fine.

He listened intently to my description of the car theft. When I'd completed the tale, he said he couldn't imagine that it had any connection to Bruce's murder. It was a thought that had never occurred to me one way or another.

"All I do, Tish, is think about Bruce and wonder who would have killed him. The motive had to be the painting. You agree, don't you?"

"I do."

"So let's think of everyone we know who knew Bruce and try to guess what motive they could have."

Hilary started counting on his fingers. He pressed his thumb with his index finger.

"One: that guy with the gallery, from Woodstock — Shaw. Motive, money. Two: the Connorses. Jean? Motive, none. Jack, money — he seems to have plenty, but they say you always want more. Did you read about him offering a reward?"

I looked blank, and Hilary went on to tell me that he'd read in the *Bennington Banner* that Jack had offered ten thousand dollars for any information about the whereabouts of the painting or the murderer.

"And not his car?"

"No, I don't think so. But that just occurred yesterday. Maybe he'll offer a second reward for that."

"Of course a reward for information about Bruce's murder could be a ploy to deflect suspicion," I said.

"But why in the world would he want the painting? And, too, I think he and Bruce sort of liked each other."

"Maybe his offer is an attempt to be a big deal, a hero. And maybe he has reason to believe his money is safe."

Hilary ignored my speculations and continued with his list of suspects.

"Where are we? Three? The improbables, of course: Sophie, no motive. George, no motive."

"Hey, wait a minute. You don't know anything about George except that he's getting his MBA at your alma mater, which makes him just dandy. He may lust after dog paintings. He could be in desperate need of money."

"That's ridiculous. He's a fine young man."

"As a detective you're a flop, Hil. You're too trusting. And as you've often advised me: Leave it to the police."

"Why don't you collect the reward, Tish? You could just turn me in. It's all my fault. I killed Bruce."

Hilary turned his head and pulled out his hankie and blew noisily.

"Oh, stop it, Hil. Self-pity isn't your style." We held hands for a while and drove in silence.

After several miles had passed, I squeezed Hil's hand and prompted, "Let's go on with the suspects. We haven't mentioned our suave storekeeper. It's possible he has better plans for his future than slicing salami for me. Motive, money."

What Sophie had told me about the attention Jeremy bestowed on Kim came to mind. Where had Lily been? Sulking with Whiskers in their car? Assuaging her anger with donuts? Or possibly planning revenge.

"How about your old pal the judge?" Possibly aided by a touch of jealousy, Hilary's voice sounded livelier. "Would he do anything at all to please his client? Who, what with all his high-falutin' talk, has to be Her Royal Highness?"

Since I didn't want to talk about Ian, I just laughed. "If it's the queen, you can bet he won't tell us. Seriously, Hil, there's a chance that the thief — the killer — was a hit man. Whoever wanted the painting could have hired someone. We read every day about violent, amoral punks who have no qualms about murdering for money. He could have lurked in the dark between all those cars and tents and waited for his chance. Done the horrible deed and was long gone before you found Bruce."

"Could be." He fell silent again for a few moments. Then, to change the subject, said "I hope you've noticed that I haven't asked you just what it was you were planning to stir up at the dog show yesterday. Please don't tell me we're going to start stealing cars."

"That'll be the day. I can't tell a Jaguar from a Tin Lizzie." We pulled in front of his house and I asked, "Do you want to come home with me, Hil?" Even though Hilary was sounding a little more cheerful, I knew depression was close at hand. I had great faith in his resilience and vitality, and I knew that time would help; but on his rung of the ladder there isn't much of it. I was glad to see his cat, Vanessa, waiting for him on the door stoop.

Hilary kissed the palm of my hand. "No, thanks, and not to worry, as the illiterati say. I'll be human tomorrow. Oh, did I tell you? I made up my mind in the hospital to get rid of everything in the barn. The fewer inanimate objects in my life, the better. I'll have all of Alice's treasures moved down and let the community club do as they wish. Though maybe you'd like something for yourself?"

"I don't have an acquisitive bone in my body, but thanks anyhow."

With his hand on the door handle, Hil said, "I thought for a while, Tish, that I didn't want to know who killed Bruce. I thought I wouldn't be able to stand looking at him. But I've changed my mind. I don't think he belongs with other decent people, and I'm going to find him."

"Maybe the cops will do it for you."

"And you?"

"Without a clue, dear, there's not much hope. All I can do is poke around and keep my eyes open."

He nodded and headed up his walk. I

don't know how, but Vanessa managed to leap into Hil's arms as he went inside.

Approaching my house, I saw Kim Hemphill rocking on the front porch. There was no way I could say "How nice to see you" and not be lying through my teeth. I needed a little yoga time and a solitary bowl of soup. "Hello, how are you?" was the best I could do.

She picked up a black trash bag leaning against the front door and asked if she could come inside to talk to me. This was a Kim I hadn't seen before. Subdued, almost diffident.

She shuffled in and at my invitation sat on the couch. Lulu, recognizing a dog person, sat beside her. Without a word of explanation she opened the plastic bag and withdrew the missing painting of the critters.

My vocal cords atrophied. I couldn't say a word. When I recovered from the shock and was able to speak, I kept silent and waited for Kim's explanation.

"I found it." In a mousy little voice, Kim told me that she had found the painting that morning on the front seat of her car.

"That's all? No note? Nothing else?"

"Nope."

"How do you think it got there? Have you an opinion?"

"Nope. Except that someone must have been sorry they took it and wanted to give it back."

It was difficult to maintain a bland expression. "That's not a very convincing story, Kim."

"It's not a story, Mrs. McWhinny; it's true. Look." She brought the picture over. "See, it's been damaged, and I hoped I could get you to fix it for me."

Kim handed me the fatal painting, and I observed two long scratches across the standing terrier's back. Then I saw the deep dent that showed up on the background. I knew that would be trickier to repair.

"Have you reported this to the police yet?"

"No, but —"

I made my hand a stop sign. "No buts. I wouldn't consider touching this canvas, wouldn't put my pinky finger on it until you tell the police." My face flushed at the thought of what a self-righteous old fake I was. "As a matter of fact," I added, "helpful fingerprints may have already been destroyed." I rose and placed the painting on the mantel. "Now, why don't you tell me what really happened?"

"It's the truth." Kim stuck her chin out. "And, sure, I'll tell the police. They'll believe me."

Kim was standing. I walked over, put my arm around her shoulders and gave her a little hug. "How about a bowl of soup, dear? I'm starving." My little hug turned into a motherly embrace as the poor child gulped and started to cry. I tried to comfort her, and I could feel her copious tears through my shirt.

I led her into the kitchen, handed her a fistful of Kleenex, and sat her down at the table. Lulu, who was always undone by tears, arranged herself in Kim's lap.

My usual and favorite kind of soup, which I took out of the icebox, had been made by dumping all the leftover cooked vegetables into a pot, along with pasta and whatever else I could find. That, plus a heavy hand with the Parmesan cheese.

Stirring the soup, my mind whirled. My two-hundred-dollar, not-so-bright idea galled me. I really didn't know what I was planning on doing with Tune's copy of the critters even when I ordered it. How many paintings did we need? Oh, well, what the hell. Then to have Kim produce the painting and her ridiculous story. What next?

By the time I put the soup bowl in front of her, she had regained her composure and was absently stroking Lulu and looking out the window at fading lilacs. Then she looked down at her fingers kneading Lulu's ears and started to talk.

During the post-dog-show party, she said, she had left the group to go get something from her father's display tent. A little statue of a couple of beagles. Bruce had been dismantling the place, and it was a mess. In seconds, she was aware of the dog painting on the ground leaning against one of the wooden tent stakes. She said it looked as though someone had thrown it there. "I knew Dad had been drinking, and he gets silly, you know. He thinks he's funny, and he never was very tidy or careful about things, anyhow. I looked behind the tent. It was dark. Dad's RV blocked out what light there may have been, and then there's that small tree there. A couple of people were standing together, talking. They were real close, just the other side of the packing boxes. I didn't call out or say anything about the painting. Didn't say anything at all. I thought maybe one of them might be a man, you know, peeing beside the tree."

"You didn't see your father?"

"Nope. It was too dark under the trees."

"Could you have seen your father if he was on the ground on the other side of the crates?"

"That's just where he must have been, but

of course I didn't know it then. So I took the painting. I was really quite mad at Dad for treating the painting that way. You know, after all the talk about how great it was and all that. So I took it back to the car and put it in the trunk and went back to join the group. Then when we heard Sophie yelling and everything and . . ." Kim bit her lip and hid behind her Kleenex for a minute. "I don't know how long we were kneeling beside Dad. Mother was there, too. Sophie and some woman were trying to help Hilary. It was like it was happening to someone else, and I was just watching."

This was not the self-assured person I'd met a few days ago.

"This is so hard for you, Kim. While I've only known your father for a short time, I'm sure you must have been devoted to him. Such a genuinely nice person."

"He was OK. I didn't see much of him and neither did my mother; he was always off on some trip, some scheme." She tugged on one of her earrings. "He brought me these from Morocco."

"Why didn't you tell the police about the painting right then and there?"

"It never even occurred to me. I thought he must have tripped and fallen. Then I heard people talking about the painting.

Even so, it took a long time to dawn on me that Dad was dead because someone wanted that painting." She sat shaking her head in disbelief. "I still can't believe it."

Kim carried Lulu over to the window and with her back to me she said, "Do you know why I want that painting? I'm going to trap whoever killed my father. I'll figure out a way. You'll see."

"I hope you will. I hope someone will. I believe you, Kim, and thank you for telling me the truth. But what I said before still holds. You must tell the police the whole story. They'll never buy the first scenario, and you, my dear, would end up in very serious trouble."

"Yeah, I guess you're right. I should have told them at the time. It was stupid of me, since the painting must belong to me now, anyhow. You will fix up the dent and the scratches? Please."

"We'll see. First, go to the police; tell all, and show them the painting."

"I'll do it this afternoon. I'm supposed to meet the detective and bring back Dad's RV."

Nodding, I led Kim into the studio, where she watched me as I repacked the critters. I taped cardboard to the back and the front of the canvas and cut down the trash bag to a manageable size, using masking tape to keep the critters safe and sound.

"Please don't tell anybody about this — you know, about the painting."

I raised two fingers, then wondered if Girl Scouts still do that to signal "word of honor."

Down deep — but not so very deep — I wished the painting was permanently missing so that I could bury my role in the whole miserable scene.

I wished Kim luck. I also wished she'd cut a larger opening in her mop of hair so that I could get a better look at her face when I spoke to her.

Fifteen

After Kim drove off, I was exhausted. I prowled around the house touching this and that and straightening up a sloppy bookshelf in Doug's den. I stretched out on the couch with my feet on the arm, admonishing myself to relax every muscle in my body. It didn't work. I was wired mentally and physically. Lulu was overjoyed when I resorted to another comforting position: sitting behind the wheel of the Isuzu.

The landscape in my particular part of the world was designed to soothe the soul and let one's spirits rise with the mountains. After a mindless scenic meander, I found myself turning into Hell's Peak Road and realized that my subconscious — or the snoop in me — had led me to the Connorses' rented house. Right away I saw their name, which had been taped on the mailbox. The driveway took a sharp turn, so I couldn't see the house. Darn it. A social call was not what I had in mind, so I couldn't very well go charging up the driveway. Then I noticed a FOR SALE sign at the driveway leading to their neighbors' house. Since both houses were no doubt placed to take advantage of the glorious view, I guessed it might be possible to peek at the Connorses' house from what I hoped would be vacated property.

When curiosity drives me beyond PRIVATE ROAD signs or unmarked driveways, I am always prepared with a heartfelt apology and the explanation that I was looking for the McWhinnys. This afternoon I was in luck. The house that was for sale was obviously empty. The lawn was unmowed, and blinds were drawn across the big east windows.

I didn't even have to get out of the car to have a clear view of the Connorses' garage and the rear of their house. And there was Jack himself with his trademark Stetson pushed back on his head, shaking hands with a much shorter man, or maybe a boy. With his other hand, Jack was stroking the radiator ornament on what appeared to be a very snappy new car.

I don't know what I expected to see, but the scene wasn't very compelling. So after a few minutes I went on my way to do some errands in the village.

My last stop was at Center Merrill's garage to fill up my thirsty chariot. So named because he was the middle child, Center's sign read CENTER'S SERVICE CENTER. As I was signing my gas bill, Jack Connors and his young friend drove up to the next pump.

"Hey Tish. How ya doin'?"

"Fine. Is that a brand spanking new car?"

"Yes, ma'am. You ever seen anything like it?"

For all I know, I'd probably seen dozens like it, but I had the grace to refrain from spoiling his fun. "That was fast, Jack. What did the insurance company do, telegraph you the money?"

Stupid question. What was fifty thousand dollars to Jack?

Suddenly I was in the middle of a mob scene. Men appeared out of nowhere. Greasy mechanics crawled out from under cars. Customers came from the auto supply store. We were surrounded. Finally I caught on. The attraction was Jack's new car.

I asked Center, who was standing by my window, if there was something special about it.

He explained that the car was one of a kind, a custom-made, four-door Jaguar convertible. He said he had never seen one before. "But, then," he said, "who'd have one of those in Vermont when you'd only have a week or so all year when you can drive around with the top down?"

"What would a car like that cost?"

"Seventy-five, a hundred thousand, two, three. Don't ask me. Ask Connors."

Of course, I really didn't give a damn what his car cost; I was just surprised at the speed with which he'd replaced the stolen Jaguar. A new car's appearance the very next day strained credibility.

The admiring group vanished as quickly as it appeared, and Jack stepped over to say good-bye to me. I told him I thought the reward he had offered to find Bruce's killer was admirable, adding, "Do you honestly think money will smoke someone out?"

"If I didn't think so, I wouldn't have done it, now, would I? Wanna bet I catch a fish? I'm betting somebody must have seen something and is gonna want to tell me. I mean, after the show ends, the consigners talk business and swap things. They're packing, going in all directions, maybe having a beer."

I interrupted. "Jean said you weren't there after the dog show."

"I don't know when I left, but I know what it's like. Been to more damn shows than I can count."

"No one can say, Jack, that you don't fill your retirement days to the hilt."

"Retired, me? A young fella like me?" Like a five-year-old he made his biceps bulge, but I refused to feel his arm and gasp in amazement. "I'm into real estate, oil wells, the storage business, waste disposal — you name it."

"Whoa! When do you have time for all that high-powered business when I always see you tearing by in a fancy car or roaring along in your truck? Let me guess. I know. You're writing a book. The secret life of a truck driver."

Jack laughed. "I'm counting Vermont cows."

"Of course, I should have known — you're a cattle rustler."

"You got it." Jack put up his hand, I think with the intention of slapping mine. Once again I wouldn't play.

New admirers appeared from nowhere and wanted to talk to Jack about his car. I said good-bye.

I drove away puzzled by Jack. Not Jack the businessman or entrepreneur or Jack the rustler, but by Jack the husband. Puzzled that someone who seemed so predictable didn't string up Ian to the nearest tree. Had he married Jean as an elegant front and

188

didn't give a darn what she did? Seemed awfully grim to me. But there was Jean, apparently quite content, and of course she'd as much as told me why: Jack was agreeable and rich. Or rich and agreeable.

At the grocery store I bought a carton of rum raisin ice cream, then headed for Goat Heaven to check progress on the house and to find out if George had done any detecting about the car theft.

Lulu's bark is somewhere between a sneeze and a snore, but at the sight of Sophie's flock of goats, she screamed with delight. I let her into the pasture to gambol with the kids and aimed for the house.

I found Sophie and George in the soon-to-be living room, which at the moment was a jackstraw tangle of lumber. George folded his stepladder. Sophie dismounted from her sawhorse, looked in my paper bag, and went to fetch utensils from the kitchen. We wasted no time attacking food meant for the gods.

In the middle of our feeding frenzy, I assessed my niece. "Glum is a possible word, Sophie, to describe your condition, right?"

"Right. Kim's going to get that monster motor home of her father's. It looks like a fucking bloodmobile, and she thinks she's going to park it right here in front of my house — my beautiful house."

"What's wrong with putting it behind the barn?" What a dumb question I'd asked. Within hours, the goats would be playing king of the mountain, removing windshield wipers and probably munching on the tires.

George remarked, "You don't seem to mind Kim's trailer." The way he'd said that made it quite clear that he was defending Kim.

It was equally clear that Sophie didn't like the message. "At least the trailer looks as though it belongs on a farm. The RV or whatever you call it looks like it belongs in an old folks' graveyard in Florida."

"Think rum raisin," I said. "You'll feel better."

George smiled at me. "Mrs. McWhinny, Sophie told me I should call you Tish. May I?"

"Of course." I appreciated his manners.

"I had a lizard named Tish when I was a kid. I love the name."

Not being overly thrilled by comparison to a lizard, I changed the subject and told them about Jack Connors's new car. George was intrigued by my description of Jack's latest acquisition. "A convertible, yes. Jag's got one this year that's a beaut."

I said I didn't know why it was a traffic

stopper except that Center had said it had four doors, for what that's worth.

George was galvanized. He almost lost his pants again as he jumped to his feet. "That I've got to see!"

I remarked that I supposed big cars were still gas guzzlers.

"Big cars? A Jag's not big" — he spoke with reverence — "but it's beautiful." Beautiful wasn't an adjective that I thought of in connection with cars, but George was starry-eyed and listened eagerly to my description of how to find his way to Hell's Peak Road. Two seconds later we watched him roar off in his minimal car.

After chuckling about men and their toys, Sophie and I roamed around the house stroking timbers and scuffing our feet through sweet-smelling curls of cedar. The last thing in the world I want to do is to inquire into Sophie's love life, so why in the world did I ask her where George slept?

She gave me a long-suffering look. "Wherever."

With that settled, I suggested that since I had heard her express an interest in seeing the new barn at the Billings Farm & Museum in Woodstock, perhaps she'd like to go there with me in the next day or two, so I could get better acquainted with Shaw and his Quadruped Art Gallery.

I think she said yes. It was hard to tell as her attention was directed up the road where Bruce's super van was coming slowly along. We watched as it pulled up in front of us.

The passenger door opened, and Kim's two huge Labs leaped over a pile of lumber and threw themselves on Sophie.

Better she than me. I would have been knocked flat on my still tender backside.

Kim wore a black metal-studded leather jacket cinched at the waist with a huge belt. She looked like a motorcycle moll or perhaps a telephone lineman.

I'm a sissy about confrontations, so I said good-bye to Sophie and hello and good-bye to Kim, who, from what I could see of her face, looked quite happy.

"Hey, Mrs. McWhinny. See you later." I reminded myself that "see you later" no longer means see you later — but seeing me was up to Kim.

At home I made iced coffee to wash away the lingering flavor of the rum-raisin orgy. I carried it with me into the den when I went to answer the telephone.

"Okay, Letitia." It was Hilary in full voice. "So tell me, what the hell are you up to?"

I just barely avoided saying, Who me? Instead I said, "I'm waiting, dear heart, for you to take a deep breath, count to ten, and tell me what the hell you're talking about."

"Phil Tune's just been here. He was trying to find your house. He had something for you, and I persuaded him to leave it with me."

Lulu cocked her head at the sound of my teeth grinding.

Hilary didn't seem to require a reply and went on to say that the boys he'd hired to take Alice's things out of the barn had appeared right after lunch. He explained in response to my questions that the boys were Londonderry friends of one of the orderlies at the hospital, who had told them to come as soon as possible.

"So," Hilary said, "it's a madhouse. I'm convinced that neither of them ever got through third grade, but they're strong and willing. Betsy Westervelt's here with helpers sorting things. Millie is here and Jean Connors is working like a Trojan and in the middle of it Tune arrives asking for you. I didn't see exactly what Tune had in the package for you, but we both know it's a painting. Knowing how devious you are, lovey, I'm feeling a little uneasy. Come clean. What goes on?"

Before I could tell Hilary that I was on my

way to collect the package, he said he had just given it to one of the boys to drop off.

"I told him to leave it at your back door. Tune asked about being paid." Hilary laughed. "I told him I thought you were good for it."

I hung up as I heard footsteps on the back porch but wasn't in time to do more than call out my thank you to a retreating back. Instantly I unwrapped the painting and was impressed with Tune's work. It was beyond my expectations. It was a perfect duplication of the would-be Landseer, minus his signature.

Now, what to do with my cute, expensive idea? Because the original had surfaced, I failed to see what use the painting would be. I had commissioned Tune to do the copy with only vague ideas and unexplored possibilities.

Instinct took care of my next move. When I heard a yoo-hoo at the front door, I quickly hid the painting in a large portfolio and shoved it in my painting rack.

Still wearing her scary black costume, Kim stood at the front door swinging the real critters as though the painting was a piece of expendable cardboard.

"Careful," I said. "That painting's probably more than a hundred years old." I took it out of its plastic trash bag and put it on the mantel. "What did the police say?"

"It took forever. One of the detectives took it to some professor at the college. She said that the painting had been too heavily restored, and even if Landseer did paint the picture, it wasn't typical of his work. I guess she didn't think much of it, so they let me take it. Of course, they're crazy. Someone wanted it enough to kill my father for it. I mean, there's just no other reason in the world anyone would have killed Dad."

"The professor may be right — it has been extensively restored." I thought of the painting as being patched up, not restored. "Why don't you put it in safe storage some-place and put the whole unhappy business behind you? Give it a couple of years, and by then you'll find it easier to decide what to do with it."

"Oh, I know what to do with it." I caught a glimpse of her determined chin. "Like I told you, I'm going to use it to trap the murderer."

When I asked just how she planned to do that, she told me that she and George had figured out a way. She planned to exhibit the painting at the Londonderry dog show and see what happened. And, no, she hadn't confided her plans to the police.

"Wait a minute, Kim." I went into the studio and returned with Tune's critters and put the painting on the mantel beside the original.

I expected Kim to be astonished, but she simply asked if I had painted it. I didn't see any particular reason to be evasive about the question and told her about Phil Tune.

"From across the room I can't tell them apart. Really cool." Kim stepped closer. "From here, say six feet, maybe I could."

"Tell you what, Kim. I'll repair the original, and why don't you take the copy in its place. That way if a thief does bite, which I doubt, the original will be safe."

Kim thanked me profusely but to my surprise rejected my offer of Tune's splendid forgery. In a way I was glad. The slighter my involvement, the better — and perhaps it was a lousy idea, anyhow.

"I hate to ask you how quickly you can fix it, but I'd like to take it up to Mr. Shaw. He wants to have it tested, too. I mean, if he verifies it, well —" she rubbed that index finger and thumb once again — "more money."

Had I been able to see her eyes I'm sure the dollar signs would have been visible. I couldn't blame her — it wasn't hard to remember how fiercely I chased a buck in my youth. Along with men and my work, money was right up there near the top of my list of priorities.

"If you want to sell the painting, why don't you just sell it to Ian Bixler? I don't know what he'd pay for it, but it could be quite a lot."

"No way. Sell it to the commander — judge — whatever he is? No way. I think he and my mother are — Well, I saw them the other day in that restaurant in Londonderry and you'd think they were married. It's disgusting. Besides, George told me that selling rare paintings could be a shady business, and I need an expert like Mr. Shaw."

I made no comment and promised to work on the painting as soon as possible. "First, I'll put some wet blotters on that dent and weigh it down overnight, and if that works, I'll just need another day or two," I said.

Watching her leave, I wondered if she'd get in a car or climb up the nearest phone pole.

Sixteen

Whoever had assessed the critters for the police department may have been a whiz, but I had to satisfy myself about the authenticity of the painting. Before I went to bed that night I called Harvey Morse. Harvey and I had gone to art school together a million years ago, and he had been a big cheese at the Clark Art Institute in Williamstown, Massachusetts. I hadn't seen or heard about him in more than a decade, so I was gratified when he answered the phone at his home in Arlington.

Sure, Harvey said, he'd love to see the would-be Landseer; he'd read about it in the papers. He said he had long since retired, but he'd be happy to give me his opinion of the painting. Harvey suggested that I bring it down to the golf links in Manchester the next morning, and he'd look at it then. He emphasized that I'd better be standing by the caddy house at 8:30, for nothing — not even his passionate love for me — would keep him from teeing off at nine o'clock.

Prompt as usual, I stood by the caddy house and looked out over the manicured fairways and God's rearranged landscape. The hell with the painting; I wished *I* were teeing off at nine.

Big, beefy Harvey's beard tickled as he kissed the air by my cheek. "Hey, sweetie, long time no see." He hugged my arm. "You still painting anyone with a checkbook who'll sit still?"

Wow. Was that what I'd been like? I didn't need to reply to his nasty crack, as Harvey was busy putting on what I call jeweler's glasses — large rectangular lenses perched far out on one's nose. He took the painting out into the sunshine, and for the next ten or fifteen minutes he mumbled to himself, squinted, frowned, and even noisily smelled the critters. He examined the back as carefully as the front, and finally he handed the canvas back to me.

"You do good work, kid." Harvey laughed. "You and Al Hirschfeld. What do you want to know? You want to know is that really Landseer's signature? Well, I'll tell you, it's as real as your signature in that pooch's tail. Is it going to make you or whoever owns it rich?" He shrugged. "Who knows, but my highly educated, feeble-minded guess is, yes, the painting's a genuine Landseer. In fact, I like it better than some of his sentimental paintings."

"You're sure, Harvey?"

"Of course I'm not sure. We'd have to use all kinds of fancy equipment to prove it, and I can no longer walk into the museum and commandeer their X-ray equipment or whatever without creating a stir. I sort of gathered that was not what you wanted."

If Harvey thought the critters were Edwin Landseer's creation, that was good enough for me.

Driving home, I felt a rush of gratitude for generous, wise old friends — one of whom was sitting on my front porch.

As Hilary slowly rose from the rocker, he seemed more annoyed than glad to see me. "Where have you been?"

"Excuse me, sir, are you from the D.A.'s office, and is this a criminal investigation?" I didn't mean to sound quite so angry, but Hilary's tone of voice unleashed some smoldering resentment. Maybe it was the feeling that I was being used — or the guilt I felt for my role in the whole tragic mess.

Maybe I was standing with my hands on my hips. I hope not.

"I'm sorry, Tish." Hilary shook his head. "I'm sorry."

By the time I pushed Hilary inside the

front door, we'd both said we were sorry a dozen times. He sat in the wing chair with Lulu, and I pulled the ottoman over beside his knees, then almost word for word told him everything that had happened in an incredibly long twenty-four-hour period that had started when I brought him home from the hospital yesterday morning.

Hilary had no interest in the house that the Connorses were renting and even less in anything to do with cars. He always liked to hear anything about Sophie — and was interested to learn that Kim had her father's fancy van. He also refused my invitation to ride with me to Woodstock. When I showed Hilary both critter paintings, he was tight-lipped. Lord knows what he thought, but he looked close to tears.

Hilary said that Betsy Westervelt, who used to be a nurse, told him he was crazy not to be in bed, painting a grim picture of how unpleasant it would be if his wound started to bleed again.

With that news, some genie conjured up a vision that thrilled us both. Ruth, pint-size, foul mouthed, and bossy, our heavenly angel, appeared at the door.

"For Christ's sake," my drill-sergeant of a house cleaner said. Frowning, Ruth took out her glasses, put them on, and studied the oversized Mickey Mouse watch that hung around her skinny wrist.

Whenever Sophie exercises her considerable vocabulary of censurable words, Hilary manages to look downright prudish, and my expletives cause him even more pain. But our language pales beside Ruth's gusty lingo, and Hilary loves every word of it.

"Holy mother of God, now I've seen everything. Here it is ten o'clock in the morning, and you're both just sitting doing nothing." She came closer and peered at us. Hilary looked awful, and I suppose these last terrible days were written in my wrinkles.

I told Ruth about Bruce and about Hilary's injury.

"I thought I heard something about the murder on the radio" — she put her hand on Hilary's cheek — "but not about you." She adored Hilary. She started up the stairs. "I'll go get the sheets."

Hilary laughed. "I guess I'm staying, Tish. Do you mind a very old man crawling into your den?"

Ruth reappeared with an armful of bed linens. "Come on, Poopsie." She managed to pull Hilary to his feet and, grabbing him around the waist, propelled him into the den.

Tidying up in the kitchen, I could hear Ruth's raucous laughter and basso rumbling from Hil. Lord knows what they were doing.

Ruth walked by me, clutching a tangle of clothing. She grinned, raising it on high like a winner. "Finally got him undressed."

Hilary and I had decided that it was thanks to a miserable, deprived childhood that Ruth had become so obsessed with a washing machine. Nothing was safe. She and I had had a tense moment just the other day about yet another cashmere sweater of mine that she had reduced to toddler size — as Hilary remarked, her size.

Oh, my Lord! I had nearly forgotten that it was the day Mabel Boland brought her pumpkin scones to the store. I flew out the door and was just in time to capture the last batch.

Recrossing the street, I paused and opened my bag to count my scones and nearly ran into George Rouse. Or, as I gathered by the sight of him with his head against the wheel of his car, he had nearly run over me.

"I could have killed you!" George waved away the scone I offered him. "Would you believe this, Tish, I think I'm onto something."

"What?" I darted around the car and got in the seat beside him. "What's up?"

"I spent all the time since I last saw you looking for Connors and gave up, finally this morning I found them in Ludlow."

"Them?" I was completely puzzled.

"Connors, with that kid. He wasn't in his new car but in his truck. They were just leaving a gas station there. I followed them home and did what you said you did — watched them from the house next door and snuck up real, real close. And Connors, I heard him say something about leaving at eleven. I missed the next thing he said, but then I heard him mention stopping at the store in Lofton. So I'm going to follow them. You better get out. They could show up anytime."

"What do you think all this cops-and-robbers stuff will prove?"

"That Connors steals expensive cars, has them made into four-door convertibles, and sells them to Miami pimps for one hundred fifty or two hundred grand apiece."

I laughed. "And if you're right, what does this unlikely business have to do with Bruce's murder and the painting?"

"Well, for one thing, the reward he's offered for information about the murder and about the painting — that must mean he wants something. Don't tell me he did that out of the goodness of his heart. If he's in some car scam, that's big business, dirty business, and he's probably not above killing someone. And how about the little guy? Bet he does what he's told — steals a painting, pulls a trigger, whatever. Anyhow, I'm going. I wanted you to know what's what. I can't find Kim or Sophie, so I hope I can touch base with you. Better hop out, pronto."

It was no time for reflection, but I couldn't help wondering: Because George mentioned Kim's name first, could that have been an indicator of his romantic leanings? Glad enough that I didn't know where he parked his shoes at night, I wondered, too, if they made a cozy trio in the evenings, discussing goats, the state of the world, whatever.

Action was in order. "Hold these." I put the bag of scones in his lap and ran into the house. Immediately, Ruth grabbed the front of my shirt in a gangster grip and hissed at me around the finger she had pressed to her lips.

"He's asleep. Look."

With amusement I peeked at the craggy mountain Hilary's body made under a sheet of rampant forget-me-nots. On one side the sheet was anchored down by Charlie's hound dog, Duke, who was quietly gnawing a rubber bone, and on the other side Lulu contributed her soporific snoring.

"Take care of him," I whispered to Ruth. I grabbed my canvas shoulder bag and, with a second thought, the binoculars, and flew out the door to George's car.

"Oh, no you don't." George reached for the door handle, but I was inside before he could stop me.

"I'm going with you." We locked eyes. George produced a massive frown while I assumed my most obstinate expression. I could almost hear Hilary saying, "I hate it when you look like that."

Then George shrugged. "Hope you won't be sorry." He drove forward and turned into Hilary's road, making a deft turn so that we were out of sight but facing the road.

Seconds later we watched Jack's flashy vehicle proceed up the road toward Manchester.

"Damn, there they are in his new car! Damn, I'd have bet my last dime Connors had a stolen car in that truck of his and was going to take it to a chop shop or whatever he does."

"Maybe," I suggested, "Jack's taking his imported toady to the bus."

"If you're right, that's where I'm going. Where that little guy goes, so go I."

"They're probably going to Idlenot for a BLT. On the other hand, if he's going to New York City, it would be a cinch for him to lose you. Or Albany — what do you know about Albany? Or, for that matter, what do you know about tailing someone?"

George said something through clenched teeth and nearly socked me in the jaw as he reached into the back seat. "My knapsack."

I pulled it into my lap. "What'll you have?"

"I'm a mess."

He was.

"There's a jacket in there. Maybe a clean polo shirt."

I dug out a dark-blue polo shirt and a presentable seersucker jacket.

"And my camera."

I saw that the camera was loaded and guessed the slick little job had set him back about four hundred dollars. "Here." I handed him the ubiquitous baseball cap. "Here's your disguise; now you can look like everybody else."

George could look like quite a few other people, I thought, examining his regular features and crisp black hair. That is, until he opened his mouth, which revealed an engaging arrangement of teeth unreformed by an orthodontist. I've always thought crooked teeth were very sexy.

I waved my wallet. "Have you any money?"

"Sophie gave me a couple of bills in case I ever come upon the kind of brass hinges she wants," George said, "but maybe you could spare a twenty or two."

I doubled his request and asked George why he thought Jack would be involved in stealing cars. Wasn't it too risky for the returns?

"Stolen cars are a vast cash crop. Three hundred a day are stolen in New York, maybe three hundred a year in Vermont. In the last ten days, a Volvo, a Mercedes, and Jack's Jag have all vanished. Say he gets three hundred thousand dollars for a four-door Jaguar convertible. Take off five grand for paying the actual thief, maybe another twenty thousand dollars to convert it —"

"Twenty thousand, that much?"

"Anything on the road has to conform to standards. There must be a lot of steel that goes into reinforcing their chassis. Then there's money for forged papers — so let's say that leaves Connors with about two hundred seventy-five thousand or so for ten days' work. Not bad."

"Could the legal owner of a car have it converted?"

"Sure, but he'd have trouble finding a guy with the know-how. He'd have to browse in the great big untaxable underworld. I mean, you won't find the head of the Boy Scouts driving one. That kid in the car must have just delivered the one he's driving. The same one you saw at Center's."

We watched Jack turn up to Route 7 just above Manchester, which convinced us he was headed for the bus stop.

I held the steering wheel while George struggled into his seersucker jacket and jammed the clean shirt in his pocket. He asked me to please drive his car back to Lofton and promised to keep in touch.

We stopped at the tourist bureau, where George jumped out, and I watched him jog down to the bus stop.

It seemed unlikely that Jack would recognize me in George's car, so I thought I'd cruise by and see if his toady really was waiting for the bus. Unfortunately, even in shoes with pointed toes I couldn't reach the floor pedals in George's car and had to waste time doing something I think we call the eagle in yoga to get the damn seat to move forward. Just as I succeeded, the bus, which always makes the town look smaller, slowed to a stop and blocked my view.

Acting on a brainstorm, I raced on ahead with the thought that I'd drive to the bus station in Bennington and beckon George to get off and tell me what if anything he had learned about Jack's boy and where he might be going.

I did some further adjusting of seats and mirrors and headed south. Reaching Bennington, I was pleased to learn that the bus wasn't due for another five minutes, so I got change for the telephone and called home.

Hilary answered and assured me I hadn't wakened him — but where the hell was I? I guessed that Ruth had added drama to my swift exit.

After listening to my news in silence, Hilary said, "Pay attention, Tish, don't interrupt. I'll tell you the whole story later. Most important, do as I say."

Hilary must have been extremely upset or he wouldn't have used words bound to raise my dander.

"Come home. Right now. George is not what he seems to be. I have just learned that he is not enrolled in the Harvard Business School. He's been lying to us — so Lord knows what he's up to. Give him a wide berth. Come home!"

On that command I said bye-bye. The bus

arrived and it was with apprehension that I waited, hoping George or his target would get out for the brief stretch allowed by the stop. But George did not appear, so I climbed into the bus and spotted him near the back. When he saw me, he bared his teeth in a fierce grimace, pulled down his cap, and slouched almost out of sight. The toady was sitting beside him. He was also wearing a cap and was looking out the window.

The bus was crowded, and dozens of eyes gave me a blank onceover.

You can't back out of a bus, or I can't. Forced to admit failure, I turned to accept the driver's proffered hand to descend.

Like most of us, I think I'm an excellent judge of character in spite of the fact that I'm frequently proven wrong. I've never been immune to charm, and altogether too often I've warmed up to someone who turned out to be a real stinker, or worse, a crook, and on a few ghastly occasions, even a murderer.

Rather forlornly, I stood watching the bus depart. George — likable, admirable George. Why had he lied to us? I wanted to weep. It wasn't the end of the world, but it was a rotten kick in the pants.

Seventeen

"He wants to go home." Ruth was shepherding Hilary toward her outsized old car. "The admiral needs to rest in his own bed without Lulu snoring and that big fleabag from across the street chewing on his dirty bone."

Ruth went back inside to collect her belongings from the house. Hilary and I had two minutes to talk before she returned and whisked him away.

I looked at my watch. There was just enough time to toast an English muffin before picking up Sophie for our excursion to the gallery in Woodstock. When the muffin was done, I slathered it with butter and shared it with Lulu on the way to Goat Heaven.

No sooner had I stopped in front of Sophie's unfinished house when the door opened, and my long-legged niece loped out to my car in a miniskirt and bangs.

Sophie with bangs? My jaw dropped. I

blinked to make sure the old orbs were working and made myself inhale deeply, a yoga practice that's supposed to calm both mind and body. It worked to a degree; at least I shut my mouth.

Vibrant, stunning Sophie, hiding her face with bangs. She looked like a television anchorwoman. I happen to know that almost all female TV reporters have foreheads, because I've seen them, but once settled into their jobs the deadening fringe descends. The unfortunate style can't be by choice. It must be by edict.

I wondered if George was at the bottom of this. I'd noticed yesterday that he was a little thin on top and was destined to become a young baldie. Maybe Sophie's bangs might somehow make him feel better, but, hey, I'm no analyst.

Sophie frowned. "George — what's happened to him? He left word on the phone that he was fine but nothing about where he was. What could he be doing? It's been two days."

"Two days?"

"Yeah, I haven't seen him since you told him about that car."

Of course, he'd been stalking Jack. I don't know what I said to Sophie, but I thought about my talk with Hilary. He said that just after I had left with George, Zeke Halstead, the grandson of a college chum, had been driving through Lofton and had asked at the post office where he could find Hilary. Charlie had hand-delivered him to my house. Turned out he was the registrar at the Harvard Business School and said in response to Hilary's inquiry that he'd never heard of George Rouse. He just happened to have his briefcase with him so he checked the student roster: no George.

Hilary thought, and I agreed, that we should keep the disturbing news to ourselves until George reappeared.

With that in mind, I put the Isuzu in gear. Kim had planned to join us on the trip, but Sophie said she needed to see the insurance people about her father's van. However, earlier I had met Ian at the Lofton store, and he seemed delighted to accept my invitation to come along. We made a quick stop at the inn to pick him up, then headed off for Woodstock.

Ian's comments on the countryside and his general chatter kept us interested and amused until just short of Woodstock, when Sophie asked what any of us knew about Leland Shaw, the stylish gallery owner.

Ian said he had met Shaw only twice: early in the day at the Bennington dog show, and then later that day he had talked with him and Jeremy Blount a while before Bruce was killed.

I had nothing to offer but remembered I'd found Shaw most unappealing when we met.

Sophie said that Kim had told her that Shaw was a friend of her father's and she liked him. "But to me," she added, "there's something fishy about the guy. I'm going to bat my eyes at him, so give me space. Maybe I can read him."

Arriving in Woodstock, we found that the Quadruped Gallery was one of several galleries on Woodstock's lively main street. We found a parking spot right out front, and when Sophie got out of the Isuzu, I realized from her hankie-size miniskirt that she was prepared to wiggle something as well as batting her eyes. It occurred to me that maybe she thought her bangs were sexy.

Leland Shaw's warm greeting to us slightly erased my earlier impression of the man.

"Contemporary prints" — Shaw gestured to the walls — "and do you know what?" We stood at attention. "No one will ever have to wonder again if paintings, prints, and drawings have the artist's genuine signature. Look." He held up a fat fountain pen. "The ink in this pen includes the DNA of one of these artists. We're all going to come to it. Gallery owners will demand that we have DNA signatures on the works we sell."

Sophie laughed. "I can see a whole new world of DNA pen thieves."

Shaw pointed out how much trouble would have been saved if Edwin Landseer had such a pen. He added that he planned to pick up Kim's painting of the critters in the next day or so to take it to Amherst for verification.

Ian asked how much Shaw expected to get for the critters if it turned out to be a Landseer.

"I was a friend of Kim's father, and I feel the greatest responsibility to get her the best possible price. Who knows what that is. I wish we knew where this painting had come from. It sort of appeared out of the blue, and I couldn't get Bruce to tell me a thing about its provenance. I keep wondering if there were other paintings where he found the terrier painting."

I almost raised my hand. Of course I was thinking of the murky Scottie painting that I had tucked away in my painting rack. Gosh, maybe George Romney or Sir Joshua Reynolds liked Scotties. I said nothing.

"From the moment Bruce told me he'd

have a surprise to show me in Bennington that day, I had a premonition it might be something really good. Let's hope they think so at Amherst."

"I'm told," Ian said, "that Kim plans to exhibit the painting at the Londonderry dog show."

"Yes." Shaw shook his head. "I'm sure you agree with me, Mrs. McWhinny, that it's a foolish thing for her to do."

"Maybe. However, I haven't heard anyone asking for my advice."

Ian said he'd like to buy the painting from Kim, but she seemed reluctant to sell.

"Well, I do have connections," Leland said, "that would be impossible to make outside of the trade."

"Tish," Sophie peered out from under her bangs, "why don't you show Commander Bixler around Woodstock. I mean, it has to be one of the loveliest towns in Vermont."

"What a smashing idea," Ian said. "We'll be back in — what, Tish, about half an hour?" He rushed me out of the shop, and once out on the sidewalk Ian laughed. "What fun it would be to have your charming niece try to worm secrets out of a body."

"Secrets. Do you really think Shaw killed Bruce and ran before he could grab the painting?" I was assuming that Kim was telling the real story, or at least some of it, and that Jean would have told Ian whatever Kim told her.

"It would obviously mean more to Shaw than to anyone else who might have stolen it. I hear a fad for pets, mainly dogs, is raging in Japan, and you know what Japanese buyers can do to the art market. On the other hand, the law must be investigating him very carefully just because he is in such a position. As Sophie would say, Tish, when we go back to the gallery, give me a little space. I promised Jean I'd find out what percent Shaw plans to take for himself if he sells the painting."

Walking around Woodstock with Ian for the next half hour was a treat. On one side of the green, huge trees almost hid the Woodstock Inn. A dozen or more colonial and federal houses claimed our attention and a turn by the bank led to my favorite ones. They were both brick, one of them painted a vanilla yellow and across the street a mansion whose coat of whitewash had weathered away to a pale, peignoir pink. I told Ian that the state's first ski tow had been built in Woodstock in 1934, turning Vermont into the skiing capital of New England.

We stood admiring some watercolors in a nearby gallery that also featured quadrupeds. Ian was taken by a black-and-white painting of a mother skunk followed by her babies. I guess I must have squawked when suddenly I was nearly pushed off the sidewalk. Thank goodness Ian's arm kept me upright.

"You!" I couldn't have looked as angry as I felt at the sight of Jack Connors.

"Sugar, I'm sorry." He struck at his chest. "I'm the clumsiest old cowpoke alive. Just been in there seein' my friend." He gestured toward Shaw's gallery. "Wouldn't you think I could leave town without knockin' into you?"

I waved away the rest of Connors's apologies as Ian steered me back to Shaw's place. I noticed Connors hadn't even acknowledged Ian's presence.

As we entered the gallery, the self-satisfied look I expected to see on Sophie's face was absent. She had shoved the bangs off her forehead to reveal a serious frown. I eschewed comment and asked if anyone else was hungry, pointing out a sidewalk café across the street.

Ian declined but urged us to go on ahead. He wanted a word with Shaw.

Remembering Ian's request to have Shaw to himself, I nodded and steered Sophie over to the café.

After Sophie ordered a pizza and I voted

for a BLT, she told me that Shaw had been hopelessly unresponsive. "Zed, zero, zilch. The guy rushed around pushing things and rearranging papers, and he answered my questions with grunts. I feel about as desirable as a dead cigar."

"Maybe he's gay."

"It would make me feel better to say he is, but honest, I wouldn't know. The only poking around I could do was in the bathroom, which was like a dressing room with stuff on shelves. I looked at his passport, which doesn't help except to tell us it's valid — but so's yours, so's mine. I mean, like, what's new? There were clothes in a closet. Guess he lives there, but I don't know where he sleeps. Said he lived a few miles out of town, but I have trouble believing him. All I know is that I can get along just fine without him in my life. He did say something about wondering what the DNA tests would reveal."

"Did the police take blood from you too, Soph?"

"Sure, from everybody who was there before they got there — guess they did others later. But I don't know."

Our lunch arrived, and we focussed our attention on the food in front of us. Eating quickly, we stood up to pay our tab and leave when out of nowhere a solid creature swayed toward us on roller blades. I yanked Sophie's arm, but instead of pulling her out of the way, I catapulted her into the path of the man I instantly recognized as a friend. They met in a terrifying embrace, nearly falling over the stone wall and into the Ottauquechee River. This seemed to be a day of collisions.

When they stopped apologizing to each other, I introduced the panting duet.

"Sandy McLaren, roving reporter, meet Sophie Beaumont, goat breeder and house builder."

With obvious amusement, Sophie took in Sandy's soccer player's legs, his mighty torso, and — what I liked best — his mile-wide smile. I wasn't as crazy about his bright-green hair.

"I can't help it, Tish," he said, running his hand over his lawn-high, lawn-colored hair. "I lost a bet."

I paid our bill, and we assembled under the Yankee Bookshop awning.

Sandy had worked for every newspaper in Vermont. He was too good and too much fun ever to be fired and clearly just loved moving around. He described himself as naturally nosy, and reported his findings in sprightly prose.

"You're just the person I wanted to see," he told me. "You keep your nose to the ground, Tish. What's with a rumor I hear about some creep in your neighborhood who's big in the porn business?"

"In Lofton?" Sophie said. "No way."

"Maybe not right in Lofton, but thereabouts. He features nubile nudes with dogs. Yuck."

"How repulsive. I hope you're wrong, Sandy."

"Really young girls?" Sophie asked. "How young?"

"You're too old — oops, sorry, poor joke. I personally love older women" — he grinned — "like you."

Sophie gave him a dirty look. "In your dreams, junior." She turned to me. "I'll go fetch our commander." She crossed the street.

Sandy made me promise to let him know the next time I came to Woodstock. "I live over there." He pointed to a funny little house next to Shaw's gallery. "I'll clean the joint up for you."

When we all got back in the car, I told Sophie that Sandy had asked me to deliver a tender message.

She laughed. "He's cute, what's the message?"

"He said, 'See you later.' How's that for purple passion?"

Ian was silent about his conversation with Shaw. He said he had led Shaw to believe that he was speaking for Kim, and had told Shaw their conversation was private.

"You mean, he wouldn't tell you what percent he would take."

Ian didn't look particularly happy. He shook his head.

We all agreed that a visit to Billings Farm would be a fine antidote to spying on Leland Shaw.

In 1871, a wealthy resident, Frederick Billings, began to import cows from the Isle of Jersey to create a bucolic haven, now open to the public and known as Billings Farm and Museum. When we arrived, Sophie went off to commune with the herd of contented Jerseys that looked like scattered scraps of ochre in the lush green meadow. A little later she joined us to explore the magnificent barns.

Ian was talking baby talk to a three-day-old colt while Sophie and I were hanging over the gate of another pen, trying to persuade a trio of calves to eat the wisps of hay we were offering.

"Those eyelashes!" Sophie gushed. "They must be two, maybe three inches long."

Then she made a volcanic sound, and I was astonished to see Jeremy Blount, who must have crept up behind us, grab Sophie around the waist and mash himself against her bottom.

"Gotcha!"

"You stupid clown!" She whipped around and I thought she was going to slap him. Instead she thrust her jaw within inches of Jeremy's face. "That's a greeting?" She stamped away, leaving me with him.

"Guess I scared her." Jeremy picked up his camera bag. "Well, back to work. Fun seeing you."

How had I ever thought our storekeeper was suave? He'd just been so insensitive and gross. I recalled Sophie's report on his behavior with Kim, stalking her at the Bennington show. . . . And then there was young, timid Lolita. Not surprisingly, I thought of what Sandy had said about the pornographic photos. No. I couldn't think that. It was just too revolting.

With the spell of our pastoral interlude broken, we piled back into the Isuzu and headed for Lofton. It would be difficult to guess what Sophie wished for when we drove through the village covered bridge. Ian didn't know he was supposed to make a wish. I wished the police would solve everything and we'd all live happily ever after.

A discussion of Jeremy's performance in the barn came up on the way home. I couldn't keep my thoughts to myself and wondered aloud if Jeremy could be the pornographer, though I denied thinking it was possible. "I don't quite see bovine creatures being the ideal subject matter for orgiastic doings, and besides, where were the nubile girls?" None of us had seen Lily on the premises, and I doubted that the classy staff at Billings Farm would condone any photographic hijinks.

"May I remind you, Tish," Ian said, "that it's no trick in this day and age to put two different photographs together. Or make double exposures and have, for instance, your Madonna sitting on the Archbishop of Canterbury's lap. If Blount is involved in such filth, the cow would be just one half of the ultimate composition. But pornography — I can't believe Blount would do such a thing. Seems like a decent chap to me."

Driving down Terrible Mountain, Ian asked Sophie if Kim and George planned to get married. I braced myself for the acid response I expected.

"Kim's in love with cows," she said. "Cows first, next dogs, and it's a toss up for third between horses and George. Besides, I think she's still stuck on that ass she divorced."

It was good to hear her amiable opinion, but I wasn't about to tempt fate by asking for amplification. My only dark thought was that George and Sophie might really fall for each other, and we'd find out George had some wicked other life. But that was borrowing trouble.

Sophie once again expressed her concern for George. I was tempted to tell them both about our bizarre outing but still managed to hold my tongue. I couldn't permit myself to think about George as a liar. I'd have to hear it from him. I hoped his quick wits and engaging manner would keep him safe on his risky tailing adventure. In fact, I could easily imagine affable George at this very moment having a beer with the target of his chase. I surreptitiously crossed my fingers and wished him luck.

I kept all my other dark thoughts safely squelched for the remainder of the drive. Back at home after a nap and a long walk with Lulu, I took my iced tea into the studio, where I removed Kim's critters from the rack and gave them a final coat of varnish. Then, remembering what Shaw had said, I took out the Scottie painting and put it up on the easel.

The painting was of no value in its present condition. It might well be covered with crankcase oil. The hell with caution, I decided, and proceeded to massage the whole thing with a generous dose of alcohol and see what — if anything — would happen.

Half an hour later I was still at work and cackling with glee when Hilary walked in.

"I've been yoo-hooing my heart out at your front door, and you didn't hear me." He stopped, "My Lord, don't tell me this is the other painting, the reject!" No response was necessary. I was beaming and probably babbling with excitement.

"Doesn't this signature say Firth, Hil?"

He took my magnifying glass. "Yup. Who's he?"

"Never heard of him, but that doesn't mean anything. There." I pointed to Secord's book on dog paintings. "Hurry. Look him up."

"Firth, Benjamin Firth . . . What do you know! The queen of England owns this painting here in the book of a pointer by Firth."

Cleaned, the painting was a knockout. The Scottie looked real enough to bark, and my efforts had even revealed a great English home in the luminous background.

"Shaw isn't going to get his hands on this

one. I know, Hil, let's take it to London our-selves. Maybe we can sell it to the queen."

We had drinks in the studio while ad-miring our prize. Later, Hilary made us a mushroom omelette surrounded by a fist-ful of watercress right out of the brook. We had great fun talking about all the ways we were going to spend the money the Scottie was going to bring us.

Hilary was afraid to end the evening the way we both would have liked. He said he refused to be hauled out of my bed by the rescue squad.

Eighteen

Puttering around the house the next day, I wondered when and if Kim would come to collect the critters or if Leland Shaw might appear instead. It was hard to believe that I'd become rather attached to the two little terriers in the painting, because I loathed the sadness they'd caused. The moment I could distance myself from them and the whole miserable business couldn't come soon enough.

Our euphoric evening had faded quickly. As I tossed in bed the night before, I knew that Hilary expected me to wave a magic wand and come up with Bruce's murderer. I reasoned that either passion or obsession had to be a part of the crime — or maybe it had been pure accident. I couldn't imagine why in the world anyone would kill Bruce for a painting that I guessed wouldn't bring more than a hundred thousand. It wasn't as though it was a Van Gogh or a Renoir.

Another concern that kept me awake was

Hilary. What if the police couldn't find the murderer? Since I was clueless, would Hil go into a tailspin and take things into his own hands? I could imagine him marching around pointing his old revolver at the chest of everyone in the doggie group who had been present when Bruce was killed; he'd probably be so wound up, he'd go berserk and shoot someone for a grammatical error.

Speak of the devil! Lulu announced Hilary's arrival, and it only took one quick look to realize that he, too, had gone way past our happy evening.

"I've been thinking, Tish, about what you told me Sandy McLaren said about a pornographer being in these parts and your thought that it could be Blount. In my opinion anyone who can do something that disgusting could probably also be a murderer."

"Oh, Hil, that's stretching. Being sleazy and being a killer are quite different."

"I don't agree, Letitia, and right now I'm going over to the store and poke around, see if he develops his films at home, and try to find just what is going on. It's sickening to think that Lily has to have anything to do with this sordid business."

"Hey, dear, you're jumping to conclusions. To start with, how are you going to get into their apartment? It's Sunday, and they're probably away."

"I'm counting on just that. And as for getting in, you're going to give me the keys."

It was distressing to see someone as reasonable as Hil act so out of character. When I refused to give him the keys — keys that are entrusted to me and to Millie — he left with a stony face and a curt good-bye.

I wanted to go chase after him and tug on his sleeve but realized that that would just enforce his resolution. At least I could observe from ringside. With a garbage bag and broom in hand, I went out to the shed, which was long overdue for a good cleaning and just happened to provide a direct view across the street to the store.

Ten minutes later I put down my broom to look at the approaching trio: Hilary with his head bent forward had his arm around a tearful Lily, and Whiskers trotted along beside them carrying a teddy bear.

Hilary caught my eye and gestured toward the house, so I led them through the back door and into the living room. Prepared to back up to his theory that food and drink helps every situation, Hilary disappeared into the kitchen, followed by Lulu and Whiskers.

Seated beside Lily on the couch, I offered

her my usual first aid: a clutch of Kleenex. "What's this all about, Lily?" My question brought on a torrent of tears, so I went to the kitchen door to ask Hilary the same question. He was shaking tea leaves out of the canister into the pot.

"The poor kid wanted to go home to see her parents. Blount said no and if she so much as mentioned it again, he'd hurt her dog. Well, not while I'm alive."

Back on the couch, Lily told me her home was in Steuben, a small town in western Pennsylvania. "He told me I'm stupid. He said my mother and father hated me and didn't want me to come home. He told me to forget about it. I'm not supposed to think — just do like he tells me." Lily blew her nose and pointed to a red swollen earlobe. "He almost twisted my ear off."

Oh, my Lord — a thief, a murderer, and a child abuser. "Does he take pictures of you, Lily?" She nodded. "Nude pictures?" She nodded again. Damned if I was going to ask her if dogs were involved. This was a case for a doctor or case worker. I had no idea of the right approach to take, but I did offer to care for her dog. "You can tell Jeremy that I thought Whiskers should go to the vet, then let me handle it. I'll make sure she's in a safe place."

That news along with tea and cinnamon toast seemed to revive the waif.

"I'm okay. I'll go back now. Jeremy won't be home till later, and he's usually in a good mood when he's been taking pictures. I'll bring Whiskers over if I have to."

We let her go with promises to call either of us if there was any trouble.

When the door closed behind Lily, Hilary said, "She let me in. Told me Jeremy mails his films to be processed. Said he's always getting his films and prints in the mail. She didn't say much, said I'd have to ask Blount anything I wanted to know. Then she got sniffly and asked me if I'd ask Kim to please leave Blount alone. She said he's all she has and she has no money — Blount doesn't give her a red cent. That heel. Then she told me he won't let her go home. You know the rest. That was quite an offer, saying you'd take the dog."

"Actually," I admitted, "I was thinking of Ruth. Ruth would keep the Bronx Zoo for you if you asked her to, and who would ever find her house?" What to do now? "Let's put the problem in Millie's lap — without any talk about pornography. I mean, I'm just guessing and don't want to be accused of slander."

Hilary poured me some more tea, then

settled into my wing chair and put his big feet on the ottoman. I relaxed as I watched him go through the ritual of filling his pipe from an old leather pouch that looked like a dead rat. Then I tried not to twitch as he tamped the tobacco firmly into the bowl with the end of my crystal letter opener. As a reformed smoker, I loved the smell of his tobacco as it drifted across the room.

"You know" — Hilary puffed — "I'm perplexed and worried about George. I wonder if Sophie's heard from him today."

"Only one way to find out." I picked up the phone, dialed Sophie, and held it out so Hilary could hear it ringing. Before the tape told me she wasn't home, I put down the receiver. "Not home."

We were quiet for a few minutes. Then Hilary said he wondered if it would do any good if he went to see Jack Connors about George. "I'll just plain ask him where that kid was going on the bus and for what purpose."

"What makes you think he'll give you a straight answer?"

Hilary looked surprised. He just automatically expected a truthful answer to a direct question. "I guess it wouldn't do much good to offer to punch him in the jaw. But" — he knocked the tobacco out of his pipe into my

Limoges teacup saucer and pulled himself out of the chair — "there's always my gun, and I haven't much to lose, whereas Connors probably thinks he'll be king of the hill for years to come."

I expressed myself very forcibly on that suggestion and, as I watched Hilary walking home, I had the clear impression that he had paid absolutely no attention to what I had said.

It wasn't until the next day that I saw Lily again. I dreaded going over to the store, but there were a couple of things I needed. The idea of having to look at Jeremy, given all the ugly thoughts about him revolving in my head, was unpleasant. It disgusted me, too, that I had been so easily taken in at first by the man's charm. What a gullible old sap I was.

"Mrs. McWhinny. A very good morning to you. Wasn't that a glorious day yesterday?" Jeremy, squeaky clean and full of good cheer, chattered on about Billings Farm and the lure of Woodstock.

Lily was paying a deliveryman and looked pink cheeked and happy. She could have posed as Miss Vermont Teenager — or, more likely, Miss Vermont String Bean. She accompanied me outside. "I want to apologize for crying yesterday, and please tell Mr.

Oats I'm sorry, too. Everything is fine; forget whatever silly things I said."

"You look like a different person today. How come?"

"Jeremy is his old self, and he says that I can do anything I want. He can be very nice, you know. His photography makes him happy."

I didn't know whether to applaud or upchuck. That rotten bastard, manipulating a child. The picture of their reconciliation was as repulsive to imagine as his abuse.

"What kind of pictures makes him happy — cows?"

Lily said Jeremy never showed her his photographs, but he'd gotten some in the mail that morning that really seemed to please him. "He said maybe we'd take a trip someplace — you know, like a honeymoon. Gotta go."

I watched Lily skip across the street to the store. Skipping! I hadn't skipped in Lord knows how long. Reflecting on this profound lapse of possibly seventy years, my eyes lighted on Millie unlocking the library door. I skipped over to talk to her.

"Well, you're light on your tootsies. Been drinking?"

"Doesn't everyone at breakfast?"

When I had talked to Millie over the

phone yesterday, I couldn't help telling her about what Sandy McLaren had said and about my surprise. Millie had a degree in social work and used to hold down some rugged urban job before she moved to Vermont and adopted the library. I told her what Lily had just said.

"Where's the market for pornographic pictures? My goodness, with smut streaming out of TV tubes and vile stuff available on a computer, you'd think it would be a dead end. Disgusting, isn't it?" Millie said.

I suggested that maybe we should sit tight and keep our fingers crossed. "Or," I said, "maybe we could find a way of telling her family where she is. Possibly they don't know."

"A runaway, yeah, could be. I'm surprised Bloomingdale's would hire a nymph like Lily."

"Perhaps they didn't. Did you check it out when we hired them?"

"I'm guilty." She cut her throat with her index finger. "No, I didn't. I guess that heel's charm blinded me. I agree with you, let's just hang in there. Keep our eyes open and hope for the best." She waved her crossed fingers at me. "You've got a guest."

I turned. It moved so silently I hadn't

even heard Jean's super van draw up behind me.

"May I let the dogs out?" she asked.

Before I could reply, three caramel Tootsie Rolls shot out of the door and surrounded Lulu. Stationary, they turned into cocker spaniels. Whatever message Lulu delivered caused the foursome to race across the street and disappear behind my house. We followed as Jean waxed eloquent about Lofton's giant maples and my blooming mountain ash.

As we came around the house we saw the dogs in my minuscule pond playing some sort of water polo with Whiskers' forgotten teddy bear. Lulu was outclassed. She can't swim and hold a teddy bear in her mouth at the same time. Her face just isn't made for it. When the foursome quit playing in the pond, Jean insisted that she had to dry her dripping, shaking trio and apologized for not having the usual supply of towels in the van. Could she use some of mine?

I don't see anything wrong with wet dogs on a warm summer day, but maybe there was something special about her champions.

"Not in there," I said. Jean had her hand on the doorknob leading into my studio, and for some reason I didn't want her to walk in and find the critters. I couldn't remember whether I'd left the painting on my easel or in the rack, but until I handed the damn thing to Kim or to Shaw, I considered the painting private business.

"Isn't this your studio?"

Acknowledging that it was, I came up with a quick lie and said I had just put a thick coat of polyurethane on the floor, and it wouldn't be dry until the next morning. I hoped she couldn't tell through the screen door that the floor was a mess. I hadn't swept the place in days.

We herded the horde into the kitchen. Jean fell to her knees and fluffed up her babies with a mountain of towels. The pack then scattered through the house. On the pretense of following her dogs to make sure they were "behaving themselves," Jean admired my living room and commented on paintings, looked at a few books, and gave the den a good going over, even peeking into the bathroom. I half expected her to open the hall closet or ask to inspect the second floor. I was convinced that the objective of her scrutiny was the painting of the critters.

Why didn't I just say, Here's the painting, so how do you like it? But something held me back.

Jean proceeded to arrange her angular body in the wing chair and cross her legs in a way that suggested a prolonged visit.

"What do you think about Leland Shaw, Tish? Kim tells me he was a friend of her father's, but I never met him."

"I've only seen him a few times. His gallery is attractive, very professional. He's probably OK. Are you concerned about him handling the painting?"

Jean shrugged. "I'm not sure Kim will make the best deal for herself; she's not very businesslike. I think that I, through Ian, or even Jack, could find a more prominent dealer. It would be foolish not to try. Let me ask you, as an artist . . ."

"Stop right there, please. I'm ill equipped to pass judgment on the painting or give advice." I leaned down to tell her assembled dogs how good they had been and hoped that Jean would catch the past tense. When she said it was time for her to leave, I was overjoyed.

When Jean was safely back in her mansion on wheels I hurried into my studio. Big as life, the painting of the critters was on my easel, and in spite of my distaste for my role in their resurrection, I got a kick out of knowing my name was embroidered in a tail. With all the work I'd done, my name should be in black letters opposite Edwin Landseer's.

Nineteen

Later in the morning I settled down in the den. I love Doug's old rolltop desk. Its capacious drawers and cubby holes create what I call my office. Somehow it makes paying bills and checking out the junk mail less of a chore.

Sitting at the desk, I tapped a front tooth with the end of my pen and wondered about Jean. Had she seen the critters as she reached for the studio door? If she had, what good would it do? I felt sure Kim wasn't about to hand the painting over to her mother.

Jean's visit had brought me up sharp in the good-housekeeping department. Not only did I shove the vacuum cleaner around in the studio, I mixed a sudsy dishpan of something that promised miracles. I was about to get on my knees and find out if miracles do happen when I was seized from behind by masculine arms like steel cables that crushed my stomach and pinned my arms to my sides. Pure animal instinct made me fight like a wildcat. I clawed at his arms and tried to pry apart his fingers, which might as well have been cast in bronze. Realizing that I was the loser in every way, with super-human effort I made myself relax every muscle in my body — or maybe I passed out.

"Hey, watch it!" a boyish voice warned, and, limp as a wet rag, I slipped through his arms and slid to the floor. Lulu squealed, and I heard the kitchen door slam.

My assailant managed to pull a dark trash bag over my head and yank it down below my waist. When I heard tape being pulled off its wheel, I screamed and kicked, but the agile brute wound tape just below my waist, leaving my hands useless by my side.

"Quiet! Just be quiet!" He put his hand over where he thought my mouth was and nearly broke my nose. "Quiet, or I'll tape your mouth."

A craven, cowering, claustrophobic spec-imen, I begged the man, "Please, oh please! Do what you want, but please, not that! Please!"

While I was still tearfully pleading, my as-sailant straddled my body, rolled me on to my stomach, and with his arms around my waist pulled me up. My bottom pressed against his thighs and my feet cleared the floor. In that inverted U shape, he dragged me out the door and across the gravel walk behind the studio door. I made another try for freedom and tried to bite through the bag at the man's legs, but it was hopeless. His arms were like a boa constrictor around my waist, and I was sure I could hear bones cracking. The pain was excruciating as he jammed me into the back of a truck or van.

A voice hissed at my captor. "What the fuck are you doing?" Then, "For Christ's sake, go, go — move!"

From the direction of his voice, I guessed he had jumped into the passenger seat. He slammed the door three times before it closed.

"Move! Go! For God's sake, move it!"

Even though I had been catapulted into hell, I made myself breathe deeply. What was the use of yelling or struggling to free myself if I died of a heart attack in the next few minutes?

With my fingers free, I pulled the trash bag as taut as possible and started to chew on the part in front of my mouth. Though it was a heavy leaf bag and not a dry cleaner's type that's recommended for suicide, I was already starting to gasp for air. While I tried to make an initial breakthrough in the plastic, I was astonished by what I heard.

The men were having a serious argument in stage whispers.

"How was I to know? For Christ's sake, don't blame me. You heard, I heard: Get the painter. So, she's the painter."

"We're fuckin' dead! I mean dead! She wasn't the painter, you fuckin' fool!"

"We can't take her back, for Christ's sake. Turn right."

At that point I gnawed a silver-dollar-sized hole in the bag, and by concentrated squirming as I gasped for breath, I brought it to my eye, which offered me a view of my feet and the mess around them.

Obviously the men had picked me up on the way to the dump. I was surrounded by garbage pails as well as bulging plastic bags and cardboard boxes full of putrid matter. The corrugated metal floor was slimy, and the smell was overwhelming. Then — oh my Lord! — I thought of the Londonderry dump. The compactor.

From my position on my side, I managed to get on my knees. I howled. The truck veered and slowed to a crawl. I yelled and screamed.

As my captor turned, through my peephole I saw his forehead and the palm of his hand before he pushed it into my face and sent me crashing on to my back. Thankfully my head hit a bag, or I would have been knocked out.

The compactor. Oh, God, what a ghastly way to die! I was silenced. All hope had flown. I could feel the tears on my face and I was shivering, maybe blubbering.

"Be quiet, lady. We're not going to kill you."

I didn't speak. My captor's promise gave me a glimmer of hope, and I tried to think. What they had seemed to imply was that I was a mistake. Who would want me? They must have been hired to get the painting. That damned painting. But maybe that wasn't the case. Maybe they did want me. Especially me.

In the sixteenth century, performers — actors, I assumed — were often kidnapped and forced to perform whatever was their specialty. Maybe the kidnappers had that in mind for me: Paint some dogs for them. No, that was insane.

If I was a mistake, I had a wild hope that they wouldn't want to have a murder on their hands and might just dump me someplace. On the other hand, if they unloaded me in the compactor, who would know what had happened to me?

"You can't leave her there," I heard the driver say.

"I know where. Just keep goin'."

In spite of my anguish, I'd been aware that we were going down a steep hill, and wondered if we were headed for Manchester. When we stopped, started, stopped, I guessed we might be where Route 11 meets 7. We turned left.

"I tell you, I know how. On account of my old man."

"You better know how to work the fuckin' thing."

What thing? I wondered. Did Manchester have a compactor?

Trying to breathe softly, I listened for any word or whisper that might tell me more about my future.

The driver blew his nose. "You better fuckin' know."

"Yeah." My captor sniffed loudly. I thought it might even be a sob.

We made some more slow turns.

"Hold it. See, he's backing out."

We came to a stop.

Breathe, breathe, I kept telling myself. Then I forgot about breathing when he said, "I've figured how to do it. I've got some more tape."

"You know you're fuckin' crazy."

Before I could think about that, the back of my prison opened, and my captor literally dived in and closed the door behind him. "Yell and you're dead, lady." His knees beside me dug into my abused ribs. He reached down and wound tape around my ankles.

I would have died then and there if he'd put tape around my head and mouth. As it was, I was close to claustrophobic panic.

Through my peephole I got another look at the top of his face and noted a pimple between his pale eyebrows. I hoped he had them all over his vile body.

"Now, listen. Back it in and open the back when all's clear. Take your time. We don't want no one to —"

"Yeah, I hear ya. This fuckin' well better work, or you're dead meat."

I visualized myself being pushed down an old-fashioned coal chute, sliding into an abandoned marble quarry or becoming part of a landfill.

The truck moved until its rear end bumped into something solid.

Again I heard the back door open and felt a touch of fresh air.

My captor roughly turned me around, and then the driver grabbed my ankles and dragged me outside. Then that same boa constrictor grip encircled me and I was dragged in that agonizingly familiar

U-shape across some gravel and even more painfully up a couple of steps.

"Let's hope the hatch is open." He let my body sag to the concrete or steel floor and knelt on one of my legs as he apparently reached forward to get something.

I couldn't stop my squeal of pain.

"Okay, here she goes."

They picked me up by my feet and shoulders and put me on a sloping surface that felt like a bed of metal marbles cold as ice and no wider than a gurney. I stopped breathing; then a fierce push on my shoulders sent me sliding feet first down a steep incline into whatever kind of hell awaited me.

Suddenly I came to a stop. From the smells and sounds I knew I was in a different world. I could hear people talking and a bell ringing. I tried to call out for help. Maybe no sound came out, but I felt a presence close to me and heard a frightened screech. A voice said, "Oh, my God!"

Then I felt hands traveling over me. I felt and heard scissors cutting the tape around my feet, and nimble hands were working around my waist. An index finger appeared in my peephole, followed by a knife. I tried to pull in my chin as my black prison was pulled aside. Two women in white were looking down at me. The light was so dazzling I peeked at them through my fingers like a child playing peek-a-boo.

The halos I expected to see were missing. Their faces were featureless mudheads against the lights. I lowered my eyes and was chilled by the sight of a large man standing just beyond my feet. He wore a bloody apron and was holding severed body parts in one hand and a huge cleaver in the other. I had a weird feeling I knew him from some other life.

"You scared us to death." One of the women in white fanned herself with her hands.

I scared them! With no luck I tried to sit up.

"We haven't used this chute in years."

Five or six other people elbowed their way into the group leaning over me. A swarthy young fellow tenderly helped me sit up.

"Oh, my God!" the first woman in white exclaimed. "Look, Helen. You know who it is. It's that lady who likes sweetbreads — Mrs. Whatshername, from Lofton."

To say that I relieved the tedium of life in the Grand Union meat department was putting it mildly. If I hadn't mustered some strength, I think they would have instantly arranged a parade and pushed me up and down the aisles in a shopping cart.

The brute with the monstrous cleaver I finally recognized as Milton, the head of the butcher shop. He put aside his gory props and bent over me, exuding nice peppermint breath.

"I'll call the rescue squad, ma'am. Then I'll call Chief Holden."

"No, please." I tried to sit up straighter and patted my hair in an effort to look less manic. "No, Milton, please don't do that."

Milton's face was not unkind, but his expression was troubled. He stepped back and put his hands on his hips and cocked his head. "This isn't some kind of a joke, is it? A stunt?"

I assured him, and the crew listening, that it wasn't. How absurd, I pointed out, to think that an old lady would let herself be trussed up, sent down a roller coaster, to end up with her feet on a mound of frozen turkey wings.

"Please don't call the police. I don't need the rescue squad. I'm bruised, but I don't think anything is broken. I don't see any blood, do you?"

We both looked me over.

"What I do want, Milton, please, is to call home. Urgently."

What a mess I made of such a simple act

when Milton handed me a portable telephone. Try as I would, I could neither focus on the numbers nor hit any button I aimed for.

"Calm down." One of the women in white put her arm around me. "You'll be all right."

My head was calm, but I was trembling like an aspen. Elsa was the name printed on the white coat of this kind helper.

"Let me do it for you." She took the little instrument from my clammy clutch, and in seconds I was talking to Charlie at the post office who told me that Hilary was in a state because my car was at my house and the vacuum cleaner was plugged in — but where was I?

"Lulu, Charlie. It's Lulu I'm worried about. Is she okay?"

"She's fine. Hilary's got her over to your house."

I hung up without explaining my absence, which, as the official town crier, must have driven Charlie wild.

Thank goodness Lulu was safe. I have a theory that there are no hypochondriacs among dog owners. They worry about their dogs before they think of themselves.

Next, I called home. Worry always turns Hilary into a raging bear — one of those Alaskan types that runs around on two feet, roaring and waving its paws. This condition renders him unfit for civilized driving, so I strenuously rejected his offer to come get me. He was so exercised that he forgot to ask me what had happened.

With Milton's phone still in my hand, I had a moment to think and realized that I was on the verge of being seriously involved with the law. Kidnapping. The FBI. Good Lord, I couldn't go through with it. The thought of having to confess to my part in patching up the painting and the whole tragic mess made me sick.

The crew dispersed when Milton suggested they get back to work. One of the women allowed as how nice it had been to see me.

Milton, clearly skeptical, was still waiting for an explanation.

I stammered through a lame fabrication. We had this experimental little theater group, and what happened today was a trial run of some young person's play that backfired. It was an embarrassing mistake and please, I begged, would he and his crew leave out my name in recounting the bizarre event?

"And Milton —" I tried to look both sincere and secretive — "I promise I will give you a complete explanation soon."

He shrugged but seemed to accept what I said. "You want my sister?"

Suddenly it dawned on me that his sister was Abby, Manchester's longtime taxicab driver. Bless Abby. She could never be type-cast as a cab driver. She said hello and good-bye, drove well, and absorbed even the most complicated directions with an under-standing nod and a smile. Bless Abby.

"Yes," I said gratefully.

Twenty

Milton and Hilary were buddies. That's how I happened to know his name. I had often been privy to their discussions about the quality and treatment of some of Milton's more esoteric provisions.

"Tish, I agree with Milton," Hilary said. "We've got to call the police. These creeps are genuine criminals."

"Cool it, Hil. I don't need a manager, I need a friend. Calm down and let's think, please." With my hands on his chest, I pushed Hilary into the wing chair.

"Whew, that effort used the last iota of energy in my beaten old bod." Carefully I folded myself onto the couch with Lulu. "First" — I isolated my index finger — "who were my two captors? Second —" I had to skip my next two fingers, which had been injured when I tried to roll over in the truck — "second, who was behind this? Who knew I had the painting?"

"Let's start with that last question, Tish.

Who did know? Of course, you didn't tell Kim about its origin."

"Of course not."

"But she knew you had the original. Who might she have told? George? Where is that boy? Oh, dear. She might've told Jack. Maybe not. Would he tell your old lover-boy, Mixler? No."

Hilary made me think of my mother, who always called any beau of mine who didn't meet with her approval by the wrong name.

Hilary went on supposing. "Her mother? Would Kim tell Jean? Maybe."

"Maybe. Anyway, these guys didn't sound like practiced criminals. I mean, who would be balmy enough to hire such incompetent young hoods? I mean, any third grader —"

"Third grader." Hilary sat up straighter. "Those boys who worked in the barn last week. They seemed harmless, but who knows? They were dense enough to do anything."

"Wasn't Jean there? At the barn?"

"In the thick of it."

We reviewed my recollections of the two men. "The only clear picture is that brief look I had at that pimple between two undistinguished eyebrows."

"So that's what we do? Look for a pimple?"

I agreed. "But not today, Hil. You know, this was a very big day at the Grand Union, and what's going to happen? Newspapers? The police? I can't really believe asking your friend Milton to put a lid on things will really work. It's too good a story. I can see it: 'Septuagenarian woman, Lofton resident, slides down Grand Union meat delivery ramp, in the interest of an amateur theatrical group.' Heaven help me!"

"I guess we'd both like to be disconnected from that damned painting." He smote his brow. "It's all my own damned fault. Why did I ever let Bruce up in the hayloft? Let's hope we're the only ones who know about that unfortunate morning."

I'd never told Hilary about showing the painting to Harvey. I knew that finding my name in the dog's tail had been a joke to Harvey, but I also knew he was far too professional to offer any comment unbidden.

"Why don't you let the police try to find these boys?"

"What could I tell them? Nothing. At least, nothing helpful except about the pimple, and a pimple isn't forever. You're going to find them Hil." He looked surprised. "With some help from me. But please, I don't have what it takes to even discuss it now. I'll program it for sack-time cerebration, and maybe we can come up with an idea or two."

Sophie burst in the door. "Well, what are you two doing?" Her aura of youthful vitality made me shrink, and her tone of voice made me feel as though I'd been caught with my hand in the cookie jar. Her dark sable eyebrows nearly met in the middle as she frowned at Hilary, who began the business of filling his pipe. She then brought her gaze to me. "What's up, gang? What's the skinny? Well?" She picked up Lulu and walked over to the fireplace, standing with her back to us.

"Something's happened," I began. "This afternoon something happened, and —"

"And I," Sophie said, turning around, "am being shut out."

When neither of us was quick-witted enough to respond, she went on. "And I'll tell you what happened. I just turned on the radio. What longtime resident of Lofton, acting as a part of an amateur theatrical group, dressed in a plastic leaf bag, made a surprise visit to the Manchester Grand Union meat department by sliding down the delivery chute?"

"So . . ." She put Lulu back on the couch and stood in front of me with her hands on her hips in what seemed to be an especially menacing stance. "So, I sez to myself, I sez, who might star in such a spectacular performance? Then I knew. It had to be my very own Aunt Letitia."

I burst into tears.

"Oh, Tish. I didn't mean to tease you." She knelt beside me. "Dumb me." Lulu sniffed along with me. "What did happen? Tell me. I'm so sorry, Tish."

From whence came the energy to describe my ordeal, I don't know, but I managed to do so without revealing why I was so determined to keep myself out of the ever-hungry press. That is, aside from a natural desire to avoid being described as a jackass. "As a matter of fact," I said, "Kim should be hoving into view any time now to take that cursed painting off to your boyfriend, Leland Shaw."

"My boyfriend? That prick?"

Hilary exhaled a cloud of smoke as if to blot out his beloved Sophie's verbiage.

"Who were these guys?"

"Don't ask. I'm through, *pau, fini, kaput.* I'm about to ascend to my bed." My effort to pull myself up was hopeless. "I'm bruised, drained, and have an acute attack of old age."

Sophie helped me. "I'll run your bath."

"And when you're through," Hilary said,

"give a bellow. You need old magic fingers to give you a therapeutic massage. I'll see to it that Kim gets the painting if she comes."

Nodding, I hobbled my way upstairs, unable to help but think as I did so how hopeless it was to try to identify someone by a pimple. I had an instant and complete picture of myself in full color, seated at a bare table, bathed by a megawatt light, being questioned by detectives Mutt and Jeff.

What proof did I have that the boys who were at Hilary's were the same two boys who kidnapped me? None, none at all. Certainly there were no fingerprints on my neck or my ankles. Nor was I wearing a polished belt buckle that might have trapped a fingerprint.

Fortunately my mental movie clicked off before I was handcuffed and led away.

After a long soak in the bathtub, I felt like a rag doll version of the wicked witch. In spite of Sophie's ministrations, I still felt a sting, as though the brutal absurdities of the day had been my fault.

Bed felt like heaven. Lulu, wiggling, announced Hilary's arrival. I knew he was trying to tiptoe, but that's a trick with size thirteen trilbys.

The bed sank under Hilary's weight. I inhaled the aloe cream he must have found in the bathroom cabinet. Massage. I slipped back into childhood and remembered my father's especially large hands that were called upon to rub a grippy child's back and my mother's cool, slim, manicured hands that were like magic on a fevered brow.

"I don't need to tell you how I felt about Alice, Tish, but dozens of times eons ago, when we were at the same parties and Doug would give you the high sign and say it was time to go home to bed, how I'd envy the lucky bugger."

"If Alice could hear you up there, she'd come down and scalp you with that favorite tomahawk of hers."

Did I say that, or did I mumble it into my pillow as I fell asleep?

Lulu stirred at my touch when I surfaced hours later. Raising my head to look at my bedside clock introduced me to the miserable fact that my head and neck could only move in unison. The difficulty of chewing a hole in my plastic prison must have made too many demands on whatever muscles or ligaments kept my head and neck together. It was torture.

Checking out the rest of my anatomy wasn't as disastrous as I expected it to be. My middle finger could have used a splint

— maybe a couple of emery boards and masking tape. I unveiled my legs, and with my toes reaching toward the ceiling examined developing patches of blue, soon to be black and blue. The only really painful portion was where my captor had knelt or fallen or maybe deliberately kicked me. Out loud I expressed to Lulu my fervent hope that I had enough energy to pursue the stupid jerks.

With hours to go before dawn, I floated into an uneasy limbo.

The smell of bacon cooking brought me to my feet. I never paid any attention to bacon before cholesterol entered our national vocabularies. But now that it was forbidden, I lusted for the crisp, fatty strips. Lust! That I could lust for anything at all at that point gave me courage.

"Have you two been here all night?"

Hilary and Sophie, coffee mugs pushed to one side, were deep in *The New York Times.*

Hilary reported that he had slept in the den, and Sophie had appeared half an hour ago.

"Kim came," he added "and I gave her the painting. The one in the frame on the easel. Right?" I nodded. "That is one jittery young woman. Of course, she's unhappy, but I had this feeling that she was looking over her shoulder all the time."

"She's probably nervous about showing the painting at the dog show," Sophie said. "I asked her 'So why do it?' She's got this idea that whoever killed her father will walk up and say, 'Here I am. Hey I did it.' Crazy."

Hilary poured me my own mug of coffee and asked, "Are you up to some sleuthing, Tish? Sophie says she's going to stake out the shopping strip around seven or eight or after work, when kids assemble."

Sophie grinned. "I'm your pimple spotter. Here." She handed me my marketing list and a pen. "Show me just where it was."

"Any pimple between the eyebrows will do. I'll have to hear a voice after that. Where shall I be?"

"In the market. Or in Hil's car. They'd recognize yours."

"At least they won't recognize me, unless they noticed my rings or my watch or were struck by my yellow sneakers. However, I will leave all such paraphernalia at home."

After a heartening breakfast of a peach, an English muffin piled high with bacon, and black coffee, I excused myself. For the life of me, I couldn't think of anyone who would have been dimwitted enough to employ those two young men, and my nerves couldn't take being part of a guessing game around the kitchen table.

Even though I had just had my nails done last Tuesday, scratching around on the floor of the truck made me look like a sloppy vampire; and thanks to having broken out in a terminal sweat in the Grand Union chute, my hair needed professional care. I decided to treat myself and take care of both.

Phyllis took one look at my disgusting nails. "Was this a fight with a bobcat, or have you been working at the dump?"

"I fell in a gravel pit, and that, my dear, is that."

She got the picture and let one of my limp hands plop in the sudsy water. "That splint," she said, "I can do a better one. And, oh, remember that friend of yours I told you had a load of paint under her nails? Name of Connors? She was here a couple of days ago."

Phyllis put a snappy bandage on my finger, and Louise gave me a great shampoo. I left the place feeling pulled together, or at least more able to cope.

With my eyes closed, I sat in the car thinking about Jean. It was certainly possible that she had fought with Bruce over the critters and raked the still-soft paint with her fingernails. But why fight over it? It was possible, too, that she had arranged yesterday's fiasco. But why?

The more I thought about it, the more convinced I was that even with sketchy evidence — the paint under her nails — and no motive, Jean was involved. I simply couldn't imagine a man hiring such dopey young men. I mean, a man might be snowed by a female, but by these guys? And I could somehow see Jean taking a chance, a long shot, leaving my place and rushing off to give the boys their orders. Maybe they worked for her, mowed the lawn, and she thought it would be simple for them to just duck in and grab the painting and run.

I certainly couldn't walk in and accuse the woman, but I could go call on her. Ask a lot of questions. Maybe rattle her a bit. Of course, I knew that I was no good at that kind of subterfuge, but I wanted to get it over with. I had to find out who and why. If Sophie and Hilary couldn't spot the pimple tonight, I knew that the pressure to turn it all over to the police would be intense.

Driving up the Connorses' driveway, I tried to ease my jitters by practicing all my breathing techniques. I didn't know how to invite Dutch courage on this fool's errand, but I hoped my slow burn of anger would see me through.

A good omen or a blessing: There was no

evidence of Jack's car or truck. I'd be no match for him. The front door was open, and I gave a Vermont yoo-hoo through the screen door. The three cocker spaniels raced to greet me.

Jean appeared behind them, red-eyed and holding a rumpled hankie in front of her face. When she saw me, her mouth opened like a Munch primal scream.

She pushed open the screen door and nearly knocked me off the front step. Grabbing my tender torso with her long arms, she said, "Oh, my God, I'm so sorry! I'm so miserable I don't know what to do." She took my hand. "Your finger, is it broken?"

I was too stunned to reply. Then to my embarrassment she started feeling me.

"Are you hurt? Did it hurt? Oh, I'm so sorry. Will you ever forgive me? No, how can you?"

At last I came to and took charge of the desperate woman. I held her elbow and steered her over to a wicker loveseat. "Sit," I commanded. The dogs sat.

Jean sank into the seat, running trembling hands through her hair. "Forgive me. Please forgive me."

I was too numb to open any channels for compassion or pity. I couldn't manufacture an indulgent smile or pat her shoulder. I just stood there.

"Why, Jean?" I finally asked. "Why this dreadful scheme when all you had to do was ask your daughter to give you the painting? At least I assume that that was your objective."

"You hate me, I know." She blew her nose and continued. "Yes, I wanted the painting for Ian. You have no idea how wonderful he's been to me. Kim wouldn't sell it to him. She was adamant."

"And you didn't mind stealing a potentially valuable painting from your own daughter?"

"The money doesn't mean anything to her. My parents set up a trust for her years ago. And Bruce's RV, she could sell that for two hundred thousand tomorrow. No, it wasn't about money. It was about making Ian happy. And everything went wrong."

"Tell me about the men who abducted me." She hesitated. "Or maybe you'd rather tell the FBI."

Jean jumped up and hugged me again, moaning more about how sorry she was. I backed away, disentangling myself.

"Do these men — or boys — have names?"

She nodded, still unable to speak.

"Were they the same boys who worked at Hilary's barn the day you helped Betsy sort the antiques?"

Jean barely nodded.

I don't know what I said, if anything. Maybe I just mumbled. I do know that I turned and dashed out the door and was in my car before she had time to react to my sudden departure. I'd learned everything I wanted to know and couldn't stand the sight of her sniveling one more split second.

Twenty-one

The telephone was ringing when I got home. The caller identified herself as a reporter from the *Bennington Banner*. I assured her that because I had no interest in amateur theatrics, I knew nothing about any events that might concern such a group. I replied to another call just minutes later, and finally sat down, carefully, to read the directions on the tube of extra-strength Ben-Gay. Idly wondering if it might be advisable to buy stock in the company, I smeared the stuff over my neck and I guess into my hair. Yuck.

I made several attempts to call Hilary, hoping to tell him about my dismal visit to Jean's. Having no luck, I gave up.

After lunch and a much needed nap, I took off for Goat Heaven. I wanted to tell Sophie about Jean so she wouldn't feel left out again.

I found Sophie sanding the cabinets in her nearly complete kitchen and proceeded to catch her up.

"She's nuts." Sophie said it half a dozen times during my rendition. "Come on down to the barn. I want your advice. I'm thinking of buying Kim's old trailer. Now that she's got the fancy one, I think she may sell this on the el cheapo side."

I followed her over, and even before she unlatched the back of Kim's trailer, I told her I thought it was a great idea. On more than one occasion when a sexy buck, like Van Goat, had a hot date, Sophie's station wagon happened to be on the fritz and she'd borrow my Trooper. I was thrilled to think that such an occasion might never arise again.

Kim's trailer was geared for dogs except behind the driver's cab, where she had built a tiny bedroom. Her clothes on hangers served as a wall between it and a work area with a small generator and shelves for boxes of canine paraphenalia. I reached for a tie hanging from a pin-up lamp.

"Is this Bruce's tie?"

"Yeah," Sophie said. "Kim painted it for her father." When she reached for the tie, I took hold of her wrist. "Don't, Soph. Wasn't Bruce wearing it the day he was murdered?"

"Yes, I think I did see it. I don't really remember. We can ask Kim."

"I'm going to camp right here until she appears. That's paint on that tie. There

269

could be fingerprints on the paint."

After the first hour of my vigil, Sophie brought me a mug of tea, and before my last gulp, Kim appeared. Her outfit leaned toward Russian with high black boots and a cossack-type tunic tightly cinched at the waist.

I don't know where Kim kept the array of costumes she wore. I suppose they weren't intended as costumes, but her odd or dramatic combinations of garments and accessories made them seem so.

Kim's changeling facade made it hard to define her looks. All I really knew about her character was her affinity for animals. She always had a dog or cat within reach, and I'd seen her in Sophie's corral leaning against a horse or scratching the goats. The child must have felt lost with her father dead and her mother married to a jocular stranger — to say nothing of watching Jean snuggling with an itinerant Brit.

Yes, Kim told me, the tie had been lying on the grass when she got to the murder scene. She'd put it in her pocket. "Dad loved it, but he was always yanking his ties off."

Had she shown it to the police? No, it had never occurred to her. She had no objection if I did. We wrapped it with care in a plastic bag.

"Now I realize you painted dalmatian spots on the tie. I vaguely remember seeing your father wearing it that day. I thought they were polka dots." Whatever the shape or size of the spots, my spirits rose to think a print might be found to identify the murderer.

I then asked her about the upcoming Londonderry dog show. Kim said that she had been enlisted by the show's committee to be responsible for road signs. She, in turn, had gotten Lily and Sophie to volunteer for other chores. "And my mother," she said, "is going to be a big help."

"How about Commander . . . Judge . . . whatever he is — Bixler," Sophie asked, "is he going to be the big cheese?"

Kim didn't seem to want to talk about Ian, so then we tried to think of what local dogs would be in the show. She said that Lily told her she was excited by the news that there was a special class for pets, with the winner to be chosen by audience applause.

Sophie, who was going to show Donder and Blitzen so that Kim could pay attention to her sales tent, once again roused the dogs to practice her skills.

"I want to get rid of all Dad's stuff," Kim said. "You can hardly turn around in that van. He even has full boxes lashed on top of the roof. Please, everyone cross your fingers for a nice day."

Sophie asked if she expected to display the fateful painting.

"Sure I will. Dog people read dog news, and I'll bet everyone at the show — the concessionaires and lots of others — will know about the Landseer. Leland says the more publicity, the better. It will help raise the price."

"To what?" Sophie asked. "One? Two? Three hundred thousand?"

Kim grinned. "He said not to talk about the money. That's his job."

"What's he going to do?" Sophie scoffed. "Stand outside the tent? I can hear him. 'You want to buy a painting for five hundred thousand? Do I hear six?' "

"You may be surprised, Sophie. This is just a little show, but, you know, a lot of people will be curious when word gets out. Lily's got someone to take her place at the store, and she's going to help me."

"Shaw won't be guarding the painting?" Sophie asked.

"Why don't you get off his case? You don't like him, I know. Well, I do," Kim said. "He knows his business, and I've never sold anything but lemonade in the year one and a pregnant cow two years ago. I need him."

Besides, he agrees with us that whoever tried to steal the painting from Dad will probably show up."

I was distracted by movement on the road. Don't ask me how a man jogging by, maybe fifty feet away, can look sexy and somehow lascivious. Of course, the impression that was telgraphed to me was re-enforced by my suspicions, or perhaps it was just my dirty mind. But Jeremy Blount had our undivided attention as he waved and disappeared from view beyond the barn.

"Our favorite pornographer has great abs." Sophie laughed. "Cute buns, too."

"You mean photographer," Kim said, "and I can tell you that man scares me."

" 'Pornographer' is the word, chum." Sophie paused as we both looked at Kim's crumbling face.

She began to gasp. "He took pictures of me, he . . ."

For the second time since meeting her, I embraced Kim. I patted her on the back and let her sob against my shoulder while Sophie and I exchanged meaningful glances in silence. Soon Sophie took over and guided Kim to the mounting stone, where the poor child sat hugging her dogs.

The heck with buying stock in Ben-Gay. What I needed was a position in Kleenex. I handed Kim a few. After another blow or two she spoke to us.

"Jeremy has pictures of me when Dad was killed, and he said that he'd give them to the police."

"Have you seen the pictures?"

"Yes, there's just me standing holding the painting that night near where I found it."

"You told the police about being there, didn't you?"

"Yup. But these pictures were all smiling and as if I was happy, and Jeremy says Dad must have been lying on the ground behind me. He said the police would think so."

"Whoa. Jeremy can't hurt you, Kim. That's blackmail, and it's perfectly ridiculous. What does he want in return for the pictures?"

"Dad's RV. But that's not the worst. Next he told me, maybe he wouldn't go to the police if I'd pose for him."

"Well," Sophie asked, "Did you?"

"Just a little."

"Like, how little?"

"He wanted me to take off my bra for a start, so I'd look naked behind the dogs."

"And were you?"

Kim's distress seemed lightened by Sophie's interest in the extent of her exposure.

"I'll leave you two to discuss the details of

the shoot. Hilary and I will figure out how to handle Blount. In the meantime, don't let him scare you, Kim. Spit in his eye." I gave Kim's shoulder a squeeze. "Why don't both of you come up for early dinner? Hil will cook for us."

The girls agreed. Now all I had to do was find the chef.

I got back in my car and raced home. Hilary was at home when I called.

"Oh, Hil, haven't I told you I've invited you to cook for Sophie and Kim and me tonight? Simple. And early. I think your assurance that all will go well will be important to Kim."

"Assurance about what?"

"I have so much to tell you, the telephone won't do. Hurry over; I'll raid the garden."

Hilary arrived an hour before dinner, fussed around in the kitchen for a few minutes, and produced drinks for the two of us. He offered a loving toast, then pulled out his ratty tobacco bag. "Please start at the beginning."

Hilary was dumbfounded when I told him about Jean. I knew why I loved him when he told me to forget about the boys, that he would deal with them without any help from the police.

He said he had written a letter to be hand

delivered by his lawyer, Zachary Pell, who knew the boys. The letter made it clear that if they ever again broke the law in any way whatsoever, their kidnapping fiasco would be brought out, and they would probably spend time in prison.

Hilary asked me what I was going to do about Jean. I replied that I had no intention of doing anything except to erase the whole scene from my already overcrowded memory.

"Hil, is it true what Jean said? That Bruce's mobile van, or whatever you call it, is worth two hundred thousand?"

"Possibly."

"You should know. What a rich old geezer you are."

"Let's not go into that, Tish. It's all past tense. I'm sitting on enough guilt about that damned painting, and I don't need a scolding from you about how I dole out my money. I mourn the boy, and I'd do it all over again."

"Sorry. That was an uncalled-for crack. I apologize. The real trouble with people like Jean is they drag you down to their level. So there. I have someone to blame for my thoughtlessness." I paused. "I know you wouldn't say anything to Kim about Jean, and I trust Sophie won't, but what do you think, Hil? Could the woman have killed Bruce? My Lord, she must have lived with him for fifteen years or more. Could he have done anything to inspire that kind of passionate hatred?"

"I guess — I mean, I know — Bruce in his lackadaisical way went through all her money, which was considerable. She left him as soon as Kim went off to college, and I honestly thought their divorce and all that was perfectly civil. But how the hell can you really know anything about someone else's marriage?"

"Ain't that the truth."

I told Hilary about Bruce's necktie with its spots and my expectations. He looked like a thundercloud when I described Kim's doings with Jeremy and his revolting threats.

"Talk about an old fool!" he said. "How could I have liked the man? We have to get Lily out of there."

"Not now. Lily is going to help Kim at the show tomorrow. Sophie is, too, and we'll be around — there's not much he can do. Let's just wait till after the dog show. Please."

We heard the girls arriving. Hilary, gallant as ever, suggested we say nothing about Jeremy in order not to embarrass Kim. However, he did tell Kim that we all expected to help her the next day and that he'd be no farther than ten feet away in case she needed him.

Dinner was totally hectic. Sophie had brought Kim's dogs along. She was trying to train them for the show by parading around the dining room table. Dear as they were, I wasn't used to dogs with broomlike tails that wag at coffee-table height. At one point during dinner I noted there were three dogs on the couch.

Hilary had concocted a heavenly mound of bow-tie pasta with sausage and red peppers and Lord knows what else. The early-summer salad greens were light enough to inhale. I'd made garlic bread and Sophie had brought a cold lemon soufflé.

"Have any of you heard from George?" Kim asked. "I'm worried about him."

"Forgot to tell you," Sophie said. "I didn't talk to him, but he left a message last night. Just said that he was okay and that he'd be back soon."

After that, Kim's excitement about the Londonderry dog show was infectious and took my mind off the distressing events of the day.

Twenty-two

I didn't look forward to it, but I made myself call the police about the dalmatian tie. I talked to Detective Apple and told him that my stiff neck was too painful for me to drive to Bennington, but I promised to have someone leave the tie at the town offices in Manchester. In fact, Sophie had offered to drop off the tie en route to Basketville to pick up a special straw hat she'd ordered for Hairy Harry, a favorite old buck whose eyes were bothering him.

Detective Apple sounded discouraged and to my surprise told me that the only clue they had from the murder was a couple of strands of hair. He said he'd be very glad if they could find prints on the tie. The Detective's friendly manner was a relief. I was afraid that our tense initial meeting might have colored his attitude toward me.

I asked, "Will I see you at our dog show Saturday?"

Apple said yes. Not only did he love dogs,

but he would be on duty in the hope that exhibiting the Landseer might provide some kind of a reaction. "I'm not happy about that young lady. First she neglected to tell us that she took the painting the day of the murder, and now the tie — a serious mistake."

When I went shopping in Londonderry on Friday, I saw the harbingers of the excitement to come. Trucks that belonged to the company responsible for raising the tent and providing whatever else a dog show required — portable toilets and the like — were backing and filling. One fellow was fastening banners to every available upright. Another couple of men were putting up a first-aid tent.

The local paper said Ian had volunteered his services as a judge, and Jean Connors was to be the judge of the toy group.

To think of a pug as a toy dismayed me. Perhaps they got that American Kennel Club designation because they were traditional court jesters. They can be seen painted with the many royal families by such artists as Goya and Velasquez. Their legs looked longer then, but now a shorter, cobbier body is the norm for a pug. Believe me, these solid critters are not toys, which my Lulu could vouch for. Sophie thought I should enter Lulu in some class, but even in an informal show a spayed bitch is unacceptable.

By nine on Saturday morning, traffic in Londonderry was appalling. After one look, I turned around and parked on the uphill dirt road to Landgrove. Hilary, my skeptical companion, said that if we should lose each other — which was a given — he could be found at the pub guzzling beer or laid out on a slab in the first-aid tent.

As in the Craftsbury Common show, there was one huge white tent that evoked thoughts of dashing knights in armor rather than powdered Pomeranians and huggable hounds. Dozens of kiosks, shelters, and small tents were spotted around the field. The trucks, vans, and motor homes were assembled by the river at the far end of the area.

"Mrs. McWhinny, I didn't recognize you under that straw hat and with those dark glasses. How are your teeth? Or should I say —" Dr. Ernie Crater chuckled — "how are your canines?"

I guess the good doctor is used to having speechless patients who are unable to comment on his witticisms.

Hilary nodded in the direction of a striking scene. Two huge harlequin great danes were lying in the shade of a station wagon attended only by a toddler in pink overalls sucking on a lollipop. Jean would've liked that! Near them, a fat woman who had succumbed to the current style of showing her belly button was putting curlers in her shih-tzu's hair. "And look over there," Hil said pointing, "I recognize Bruce's awning."

We elbowed our way through a small crowd that was looking at the painting of the critters.

Kim got high marks for strategy. The placement was such that no one could reach the painting without climbing three steps into the van. It had been hung just inside the van against a dark background, with the large open doorway serving as a frame.

Even while I was observing all of this, Hilary had found a canvas director's chair and planted himself in it right beside the steps.

"Now," he said to Lily who had been sitting on the steps, "you run along and have fun. I'll hold the fort."

Lily kissed his cheek and went loping off with a beribboned Whiskers at her side.

Sophie appeared with Donder and Blitzen in tow. "Pretty cool setup. And just between us," she whispered, "Kim says that that painting is a copy of the original. Can you believe it? The real one's in Shaw's vault in Woodstock."

My mouth was glued shut. A copy. Had someone stolen *my* copy? And then I remembered Kim long ago saying that she and George had figured out how to display the critters. Light dawned. It had to be George — or was it Shaw?

Phil Tune, the rat. I waved a quick goodbye to Sophie and bumped into people and dogs as I searched for Tune's display tent.

When I finally located it, two or three people were talking to the scruffy fellow. Smoke as usual blurred his features, but he saw me and grinned as best one can with a butt in one's mouth.

I removed my dark glasses so he could get the full impact of the venom in my eyes. I squared my jaw and may even have hissed. At least the others drifted away.

"Well, Mr. Tune, tricky Mr. Tune. Tell me all about it. How many Landseers have you painted in the last two weeks?"

He beamed. "Just two. Honest. Pretty good, aren't they?"

"For whom did you make the other copy?"

The rascal beamed even brighter. "That would be telling."

Because my position wasn't exactly holy,

what could I do or say to this unrepentant sneak? "You signed Landseer's name on your other copy?"

"No ma'am, I'm not crazy. Like yours, I leave that up to the customer. Hey, I'm just making an honest living." He leaned over a cooler. "Want a beer?"

Even a biting departure line was denied me by a bevy of Lofton friends who suddenly surged into Tune's tent. I fought my way back out.

There was no way I could stay angry wandering among the dizzy assortment of setters, pointers, airedales, and Sealyhams — not to mention one snarling, mountainous komondor. At the other end of the scale was a pair of chihuahaus no bigger than my winter mittens. The eavesdropping was splendid, too. "They've been feeding him beets to make his coat redder." That accusation from a woman hugging her henna chow. A dapper fellow, maybe a handler, said to his lookalike, "Those bulldog people are terrible drinkers." I also caught a toast being made by a glamorous young thing to the man beside her. "And I learned all about corgies from you, darling."

When I realized I was thinking about adopting, buying, or stealing one out of every three dogs, I knew it was time to find

Hilary and go home for lunch.

I found him still doing sentry duty but clearly tired. Then I told him what Sophie had said.

"You mean," Hilary said, "I've been guarding a forgery all morning? Even if it was the original, who would be stupid enough to try to steal it in broad daylight? Lord knows how many police dogs will be watching."

"I don't know. Kim wants to lure a buyer. I can tell you that if Shaw sells it for a hefty price, I hope the buyer makes out a separate check for Kim."

"You don't trust him?"

"Who knows? Yesterday I read about a New York lawyer dealing with the disposition of a huge art collection who said the worst thugs he ever ran into were in the art business. We're babes in the woods."

"I'll be glad when today is over — it's a sorry and sad chapter in my life."

Lily had resumed and now emerged from the van. "Are you about to go?" she asked. "Kim's inside and said I could leave. May I go with you? Whiskers has been up-chucking, and I think I'd better take her home."

"Of course," I replied, hoping the up-chucking had run its course — at least until we got back to Lofton.

We had nearly reached my car when Jeremy ran up behind us and grabbed Lily's arm. "Where are you taking my girl?" The man was livid.

"The dog is sick," Hilary said. "We . . ."

But Blount didn't wait for Hilary to finish speaking. We watched Jeremy pull Lily and Whiskers down the hill and push them both into the Mercedes.

"What's the matter with him?" Hilary snarled. He sat fuming beside me as we drove home.

Arriving home, we found that Jeremy had taken the shortcut. The Mercedes was parked beside the store. Hilda, arms akimbo, was standing by the door. I imagined that Jeremy had swept by her and that he and Lily were upstairs. Hilary and I shook our heads and went into my house.

Hil cheered up when I brought in a tray with tall glases of iced coffee and cucumber sandwiches I had made that morning.

"Here." I tossed him a couple of handkerchiefs that I had left on the end table. "These are from the other day when Ruth did your laundry. She put them in my drawer by mistake."

"This dinky one isn't mine." He held it up. "It's got a gender, but not mine. Initials say JHE. Who would that be?"

"Hemphill," I guessed, "and J is for Jean."

Hilary couldn't recall Jean's maiden name but remembered using a hankie he'd found at the murder scene to staunch the flow of his own blood. "Look, I must have put it in my pocket. It's not uniformly white — this grayish part could be a blood stain. Tish, please don't even think. Just give this to the police. Please."

"You give it to them. They may be a little tired of me." I added that I was sure Sophie would forgive us for not watching her trot around the ring and that I had no intention of going back to the dog show until later in the day, maybe four o'clock or so.

Before I was through speaking, Hilary was asleep with his feet on the ottoman, and I spent an hour on my chaise longue with my neck on a heating pad.

When I came downstairs Hilary had gone, and I sensed something was going on outside. I opened the door and saw an old fellow in what looked like a repairman's uniform leaning on the hood of his car, writing something.

OFFICE OF THE SHERIFF was printed on the car door. I noticed the license plates were from Pennsylvania.

I walked over and asked the man where he

was from. He responded with the name of some county, Sage, I believe he said. I offered to help him find whomever he was looking for.

"Nope. I'm just waiting on him. He'll be out. Not to worry."

Then another man with an official-looking patch on his breast pocket opened the door of the store to let Jeremy Blount walk by him. Jeremy was dressed smartly and was carrying his suitcase and camera bag. He saw me and waved jauntily. I was astonished.

The sheriff opened the car's back door, and with another wave, the debonair pornographer sank out of sight.

I watched the car leave. Then I saw Lily hanging on to the pillars supporting the store's front porch. Alongside, Hilary kept her from sliding to the ground with a grip on the back of her belt. Whiskers was happily romping with Lucifer and Duke, helping to bring the scene back closer to normal.

"What," I asked Hil, "was that all about?"

"I feel as though I've been part of a not-so-funny comedy of errors. I came over to see how things were going. Lily asked me to hold the fort here while she unpacked something in the storeroom. Hilda and Joe were out in back, but Blount wasn't around. In walks this fellow who instantly shows me his badge — huge, looked like a kid's toy — says he's from Sage County, Pennsylvania, and asks if I'm Blount. I assured him that not only was I not Jeremy Blount, but I definitely wasn't a pornograher."

" 'A pornographer?' the guy said. He looked elated; guess he thought he'd caught a big one. At that point Lily came in and told us Blount was upstairs. The sheriff inspected Lily over his specs, took an envelope out of his pocket, and said it was a warrant and that his job was to escort Blount back to Sage County, where he would face charges under the Mann Act. He acted as though he expected a round of applause, leered at Lily, and marched upstairs."

"The Mann Act? What a quaint idea. I thought it vanished with the sexual revolution. No more mention of pornography when the sheriff took Blount out?"

Hil shook his head.

I tugged his arm and softly asked what was going to happen to Lily. She may have heard me. In any event, she said she wanted to finish her job and stay for the rest of the summer. But, she said, "I'd be scared to live alone here."

"Don't worry dear, we'll work something out. Maybe you could move in with Sophie or Kim — we'll see. Why was Jeremy so angry?"

"He didn't want me to be with Kim. At least I think that was it."

When we returned to the dog show, I was delighted to find a parking place right in front of the bank. I expected the activities to be winding down; instead, the joint was jumping. Both gaiety and tension were in the air. Since ninety-five percent of the dogs at any show are bound to be losers, the hopefuls, as Sophie would say, are really wired.

An Irish wolfhound seemed to dominate the group aspiring to best in show. I would have put my money on a small black dachshund who looked determined to win, and dachshunds usually get their way.

Shortly after that, Ian, with great dignity, proved me correct by bestowing a blue ribbon and an outsize silver cup to the satisfied little creature, Sir Gerald of Whipdedoodle Farm.

I ducked out of bedlam and ran right into George Rouse. I really didn't know George all that well, but I hugged him like a grandma.

"No questions now. Where's Kim's van?"

We worked our way through prancing,

yapping, panting dogs who must have been relieved that the long day was over and hoped for gustatory rewards.

Framed by the van door, Leland Shaw was removing the terrier painting from its own frame. We watched him come down the steps and pause to say something to Kim, who patted him on the back.

Tune's performance had made me eager to get a close look at the painting, so while George twirled Kim around and enveloped her in a bear hug, for a split second I got my nose within six inches of the canvas that Shaw was slipping into a cardboard carrier. It doesn't take even a split second to recognize one's own name, and there was TISH entwined in the terrier's tail.

Shaw said good-bye. Kim smiled and waved from behind George's shoulder while I watched the gallery owner vanish behind the van, en route, I expected, to his car.

Tall as Hilary is, it doesn't take long to lose him. He was nowhere in sight.

Ian, who was just coming out of the big tent, waved and made a beeline for me. Taking my arm, he pulled me aside and asked, "Did you just see Shaw leaving with that painting of the terriers?"

"Yes, I did. That's why I'm sort of in a swivet."

"Promise not to say boo, Tish, but that's not the original painting by Landseer; it's a copy."

"You're wrong, my friend; it's the real McCoy."

"I hate to contradict you, Letitia, but you're mistaken."

I had to close my eyes for a second and grit my teeth. Why should I insist that I was right? Why tell him about my name in the dog's tail? Maybe Ian had some arrangement with Kim — or Lord knows what. I could almost hear Sophie saying, "Butt out." Good advice.

"Hey!" Jack Connors's voice drowned out all further thoughts. "Where's that gallery fella going with my painting?" He pushed back his Stetson to reveal a furrowed brow.

"Your painting?" Ian smirked. "You don't say, old chap."

Detective Apple had appeared with no fanfare but stepped up on the van steps and, in a voice some of us could hear, addressed Kim.

"Please, young lady." He put his hand on Kim's arm. "You are under arrest for withholding evidence and denying the authorities other pertinent information."

"And maybe," a voice said from someone near the van, "patricide."

Kim screamed and beat Detective Apple's arm. "Are you fucking crazy? I haven't done anything! You think I'd kill my own father?"

I caught Hilary's eye and beckoned. He walked right by me and I saw him hand the detective Jean's handkerchief. Only then did he join me.

Sophie saw us sneaking behind Bruce's van and broke away from the brawling scene. "Quiet — quiet," I said. "And hurry." Hurrah for Sophie; she didn't say a word. Just trotted along beside us with two soaking wet Labradors in tow.

"They were so tired," she told us breathlessly, "I let them have a swim in the river."

"Lord knows where Shaw's gone," I said, "but we're going to find him. That's the real Landseer he's got."

We piled into the Isuzu, Sophie behind the wheel and Hilary in back with the two huge, loving, wet dogs.

"Pray that Sandy McLaren is home." I reached for Sophie's cellular phone from which she was inseparable. I got Sandy's number from information and thank goodness he answered right away. "This is an emergency, Sandy. I think Leland Shaw is trying to leave the state or the country. Run next door and look in the gallery windows. I'll hold on."

"Better yet," Sandy said, "I still have the keys he gave me a few days ago for the UPS guy."

The only sound while I waited for Sandy to return came from the dogs in the back seat kissing Hilary.

"He's flown the coop," Sandy reported as he came back on the line. "Stacks of prints with labels on them for this or that gallery. No personal stuff. Some notes on the pad by the wall telephone: Kim, eight point thirty, Howard twelve, Bradley eight plus. I know who Kim is — Howard and Bradley I don't know."

"I love you, Sandy. Good-bye."

"Okay, Soph. Let her rip — we're off to Hartford. We're going to surprise Shaw at the airport."

"That's a stretch, Tish," Hilary said. "I hope you're right. You think Bradley is Bradley International Airport? Maybe you should call the detective."

"Kim and Connors and Ian are probably still stirring it up — and what can Apple do? Shaw has Kim's painting, with her blessing. It's no crime. He'll say he's going to show it to a prospective buyer. But me, I'm suspicious. I think he's taking off for keeps."

Hil said, "That detective thanked me for the hankie; said the only evidence they had was some strands of hair — but they found out it didn't match anyone's DNA."

"What color hair?" Sophie asked.

"Blond."

We were quiet for a minute. "Great minds," I said. "We're thinking the same thing, aren't we, Sophie?"

Hilary added that he had a great mind, too. "I now recall some crack you made about Shaw's wig. Of course a hair from his wig wouldn't match that bastard's DNA."

"Bastard is right," Sophie said. "Actually that was a pretty good rug of his. At least good enough to slip by the fuzz. What was going on when we left, Tish? I wouldn't want to be standing between Connors and the commander. They were bristling like a couple of cocks."

"They both seem to think they own the Landseer. What a mess."

"Yes, Letitia, that was a timely exit we made. Did I see George Rouse?"

Sophie and I both talked at once but neither of us had said more than two words to George.

I proceeded to tell her about George tailing Connors's young toady to Lord knows where.

"What a saga! He must have plenty to say about it. The guy may be the murderer, a hit man, murder for pay. But one thing at a time. What are we going to do, Coach, if we do find Shaw? Tackle him?"

"I'm thinking." Which I was as I scrunched down in my seat and closed my eyes.

"Just relax, gang," Sophie said, "and pretend you're in Indianapolis."

Twenty-three

At the main entrance of Bradley International near Hartford, Connecticut, Sophie came to a dramatic stop, jumped out of the car, and ran inside. I slid into the driver's seat and drove into the nearest parking lot.

I gently prodded Hilary awake. "Come on. Hurry. Please make sure the doors are locked, and leave enough air for the dogs. And hurry, Hil, hurry! It's almost eight."

Scurrying out of the Trooper, I raced into the terminal and fumbled for the right glasses to read the information on the first flight screen I could find. A hollow voice on the PA system said something about boarding a flight to Atlanta. There seemed to be quite a few flights about to leave.

Hilary pulled up behind me as we heard Sophie let loose with one of her fingers-in-the-mouth, ear-splitting whistles.

"Over here, quick!" she called. "He's at gate six."

Then, because I imagine she was afraid

we couldn't move fast enough, she dashed over and got between us, took a firm grip on our arms, and propelled us down an endless aisle and through security screening. Hilary's keys slowed him down, but Sophie and I ran on to gate six, where I could see a line forming to board the plane.

"There he is — there in the middle."

"Where?" Hilary shaded his eyes with his hand. "I don't see him."

"Skinny, bald guy, with the blue blazer."

Then I saw the cardboard picture carrier. But for it, I would never have recognized Shaw without his wig. I remembered my great Aunt Sally Wainright Bell who had had two wigs, which in those days were always referred to as transformations, and indeed the wig had transformed Leland Shaw. I yanked Sophie's arm. "Bump into him."

"What?"

"Shaw. Bump into him. Stop him. Hug him, step on his toes, push him. Just do it — now!"

I don't know which of my suggestions Sophie chose, bless her, but as a result of whatever she did, Shaw nearly fell over backward. His ticket flew up in the air and the painting skidded across the polished floor.

Sophie, full of apologies, helped a fuming

Shaw to his feet while dear old Aunt Tish patted his arm and adjusted his jacket. All these tender ministrations were accomplished while I was swiveling my head around looking for an airport guard or a cop.

Thanks to the powers that be, I spotted a uniformed officer looking in our direction from the next entry gate. I ran over to him, waving my arms and giving a stellar imitation of hysteria. I told him my wallet had been stolen by the bald man who had been carrying the cardboard case.

Dragging the reluctant officer toward Shaw, I pointed. "He's the one. Don't let him get away." At a lower decibel level I repeatedly yelled help to a rapt audience.

The airport officer pulled himself together, took charge of Shaw, and ordered him to empty his pockets.

Shaw, snarling at me, put his hand in his jacket pocket and, with a look of utter horror, withdrew not one, but two wallets.

The small crowd silently stared at the damning evidence.

A great roar from Hilary further mesmerized the group as he announced that his wallet, too, had been stolen. "And, goddammit, there it is! In his hand!"

Hilary simmered down quickly when he

apparently realized my sleight-of-hand trick.

I turned from the bizarre scene to ask Sophie to call the Bennington police and see if she could get through to Detective Apple to tell him about everything, including Shaw's wig and Lily's remark about seeing a bald man at the murder scene. Then I stopped. "You didn't tell me, Sophie. How is it that Lily saw Shaw? Where was she?"

"She was weeping in Bruce's van — wanted him to get Kim to quit making moves on Jeremy."

I was about to comment when the officer began waving me over.

"Hurry, dear. The officer wants us." Hilary and I were led to the door of a small office. I stopped and refused to go inside. "No, officer, I'm not the thief. I will not be subjected to that man's vituperative wrath."

Shaw was sputtering like a firecracker. "That woman! That crazy old bitch!"

The policeman cocked an eyebrow at me, but I remained adamant. "I don't have to take that abuse, officer. You have our wallets. We're not going anyplace. We'll wait outside."

Hilary jumped in. "Tish — leave it to me; calm down." He spread his big hands and advised me to calm down at least half a dozen more times, then joined Shaw and the

300

officer inside the room.

Sinking into the nearest row chair, I wondered if I would be jailed instead of Shaw. All I cared about was the speed with which Apple could send someone to take over the situation. It troubled me that I couldn't prove a thing against Shaw, and I hated the idea of spending my dwindling years working on a chain gang because of my act of desperation.

Sophie spoke from behind me. "I got him. Detective Apple's sending someone here from the Hartford police. But listen. Some other guy at the Bennington police station said they found out from Shaw's landlord that he was way behind in his rent, and the cleaning man, Howard something, was sure Shaw had left permanently. Evidently they found other evidence, too. So, how about that?"

I expelled a ton of guilt, doubt, and fright in the longest sigh of my life. What a relief!

Within minutes a tidy young man jogged by us and into the small office. In two more minutes he reappeared, carrying the painting case and prodding Shaw, who was trying to hide his handcuffs. They disappeared without so much as a glance in my direction, thank goodness.

The airport officer and Hilary ambled

over, all smiles, and Hilary bent close to my ear. "Here's your stolen wallet, you tricky 'old bitch.' "

My suggestion that we find a motel and call it quits was vetoed. Hilary led us to an airport tavern where he and I each had a drink and grilled cheese sandwiches, while our self-designated driver ate two hamburgers and ordered two more to go for the dogs.

Picking myself up from the tavern banquette took almost more energy than I had left. However, since spending the night there was neither practical nor inviting, I managed to make my way back outside to the parking lot — ably assisted by Sophie and Hilary on either side of me — and sank gratefully into the passenger seat of the Isuzu.

After a quiet half hour in the car, Hilary said that it was clear to him that Shaw was the murderer and the motive was his urgent need for money.

"What's new?" Sophie asked as she passed a double trailer truck, going ninety. "Kim will be the loser, but, then, she hasn't owned the painting long enough to miss it."

I reflected on her words. The next thing I knew, Hilary was saying good night to us at his door. I barely remember going to bed.

It wasn't until late the next afternoon that anyone showed up at my house. Detective Apple arrived first. I'd never given the detective my full attention before. I was reassured to see that the few lines in his round face conveyed an amiable demeanor. His blue eyes behind wire-rimmed glasses seemed to have a little sparkle, and his handshake earned him an A-plus.

Detective Apple put down the now very familiar cardboard carrier. "That was a dangerous and daring maneuver of yours at the airport, Mrs. McWhinny. We are, of course, glad you apprehended Shaw before he could leave. But please, lady, sit the rest of this case out on one of those rocking chairs on your front porch."

"The rest of it?" Hilary had arrived and was listening at the front door. "What else is there, officer? We were under the impression that the case was closed."

The detective shrugged. "That handkerchief you gave me must have been covered with your blood. Sir, the victim didn't bleed. Unlike an ice pick, the increasing size of the awl's blade acted as a stopper. Mrs. Connors said the handkerchief did belong to her. We've had the first DNA tests on the blond hairs we found in Shaw's basin. While they're not conclusive yet, they point strongly at him. The tie your niece delivered has —"

The detective stopped short at the sudden commotion outside.

Jack Connors sounded as though he'd forgotten to dismount from his bronco before he came up the porch steps. I could have skewered him myself for interrupting Apple. He was dragging his reluctant, red-eyed wife. Their noisy progress was slowed by the fact that Jean was the object of a tug-of-war — Ian had a firm grip on her other hand. Kim added to the din by hurling epithets at Ian as she came in. I assumed that someone had posted bail for her, for Detective Apple seemed unconcerned by her entrance. Her dogs, barking loudly, added to the confusion. George, looking bemused, brought up the rear. Seconds later, Lily, a panting Whiskers, and Sophie appeared.

"Do come in," I said with unsurpassed sarcasm. Jean suddenly broke away from the men and stunned us all by walking over to Detective Apple and pounding him on the chest. "I did it, officer! I killed him!" Almost yelling her confession, she backed the surprised detective into a corner. She held her wrists together, inviting handcuffs.

"No, don't believe her! She didn't." Connors pulled Jean back from Detective

Apple, thus saving my favorite standing lamp.

We were a silent captive audience when Jean spoke in a shaky voice. "Bruce spent all my money. Everything I had. Smiling all the while. Everyone thought Bruce was so much fun. 'Isn't he cute,' they'd say — while he was going through more than two million dollars. My dollars. He owed me that painting."

Detective Apple raised his hand. "You say you did it, ma'am. Where did you get the awl?"

"The awl?" She looked puzzled. "Oh, Bruce had it in his hand. He was drunk. He said since I was so mad at him, why didn't I just kill him? All I wanted was the painting. He was laughing. I got mad. I pushed him. He fell over."

Connors interrupted, "And I found her standing there. She didn't do anything, Captain, she's just upset. Hell, Bruce was getting up when I took her away."

He put an arm around Jean, and they backed away, letting Detective Apple out of the corner. I guess I lack the milk of human kindness, but I had no sympathy for the woman, nor did I really believe her.

"It's ridiculous to even think that my mother could have killed my father," Kim said. "I'll tell you who it must have been. It was him." She pointed at Ian. "He probably put Mother up to it. She didn't care about the painting; he did. He wanted it for the queen of England or whoever he works for. He's the one!"

"I'm hurt and offended." Ian looked as though he was going to cry. "Deeply offended by the inference that I would do violence to your father, Kim. Or, for that matter, to anybody. You'll be gratified to know that the painting of the terriers attributed to Landseer — the painting that has been the cause of all this misery — left early this week by diplomatic courier for England. I negotiated an excellent price with Leland Shaw. A financial agreement that should please you, Kim."

You could hear the proverbial pin drop. Detective Apple busied himself opening the cardboard carrying case and carefully he drew out the critters. My original critters.

"Mrs. McWhinny" — he handed the painting to me — "you're the artist. Is this the Landseer, or is it a copy?"

I barely had to glance at it. "I told you, Ian — and yes, Detective Apple — this is the original Landseer."

White-faced, Ian took the painting from me and held it in shaking hands.

306

"May I?" I reclaimed the canvas and turned it upside down. "See?" I pointed to my name entwined in the terrier's tail.

Ian, looking as though he had shrunk two sizes, sank into the wing chair.

With the exception of George and Hilary, everyone else seemed to have lost the use of their legs. Jack and Jean, still joined, thudded onto the window seat. Kim, with her mouth open, straddled the ottoman. Detective Apple sat in a straight chair by the window. The glue in my knees had evaporated, too, and I landed on the couch with Sophie, who was sandwiched between Kim's dogs — Lily, Whiskers, and Lulu. I personally know people who have dogs that sit on the floor, but none in Lofton.

George, still on his feet, strode into the kitchen and returned with two glasses of water. He handed one to Jean and put Ian's fingers around the other.

Hilary, who had moved over to the bar, placed a welcome drink for me on the end table.

Solemnly, rather like a Boy Scout leader, George stood in front of the fireplace. "Not to change the subject . . ." He smiled. My guess was that none of us was quite sure what the subject was. "This" — he waved a paper in the air — "is a copy of all information my uncle's insurance company has compiled to be turned over to the law. This is for you, Detective Apple."

Twenty-four

Watching a strangely silent Jack Connors leave, Ian tried to get up, then thought better of it.

Kim went over to her mother and, whispering, urged her outside, where I could hear them moving the rocking chairs closer together.

George cleared his throat as though preparing to deliver another bombshell, but Hilary took hold of his shoulder. "Son, please wait. It's all too much for my addled old bean. Let me ask Detective Apple what he was saying when I came in a few minutes ago."

"About the dalmatian tie," I prompted.

"Right. We found a good fingerprint on one of the painted areas of the dog tie that belonged to the deceased and were able to identify it as Shaw's. Then, this young lady here, Lily, who was in the deceased's motor home, saw first Mrs. Connors grappling with her ex-husband over the painting, then saw Mr. Connors leading her away. The last person she saw with the deceased was a bald-headed man, and from a picture of him without his wig, faxed to us by the Hartford police, she identified him as the man she had seen: Leland Shaw."

"So he is the murderer?" Hilary asked.

"I think that's a reasonable assumption to make. But, as you know, the final word is up to the court. Now, if you'll excuse me." Detective Apple spoke with George for a few minutes and departed.

I looked at Ian and was saddened to see him leaning over with his head in his hands.

Sophie moved over to sit on the arm of his chair. Making sympathetic sounds, she rested her hand on his shoulder. "Poor guy," she said to us. "He's really been taken to the cleaners."

"How could you have let Shaw fool you, Ian?" I couldn't help asking the question.

"Because I'm a stupid, gullible idiot. Shaw had both the original and a copy of the painting when I saw him in Woodstock earlier this week. He had done an amazing job on the copy. I mean, beyond having it painted, he antiqued the back of it, and the signature was perfect. He put them both up unframed on that big easel, and it was my idea to send my client the painting then and there."

"You paid him for it?" George asked wide-eyed, "and just walked away?"

"No, no. As I said, it was my plan to send the painting off with a diplomatic courier; I know someone in Boston who, with a minimum of red tape, would take it to London the next day. I watched Shaw wrap it. We went to the post office together. I even paid the charge. I was confident the painting was safely on its way." He paused to shake his head a few times. "I cabled my bank to transfer funds to what Shaw called the art dealer's account in a Swiss bank. You know, just a number, really. I told Shaw I wanted to pay his commission and pay Kim for the painting separately. Shaw said no, that he and Kim had an agreement that he would handle everything." Poor Ian hit his forehead with the palm of his hand.

"You mean," Hilary asked, "Shaw slipped the copy into the box and you yourself mailed it?"

Ian nodded. "I'm afraid I did."

"I guess that was a pretty damn good copy." George beamed. "It was one that I ordered from some clever guy who paints dogs —"

It's a good thing Sophie was both quick

and strong as she clutched Ian and blocked his force as he lunged out of his chair and dived at George. Perhaps Ian's intention was to roar at George at close range, but he managed to knock him backward when he tripped over my brass fireplace fender.

Ian was instantly remorseful and full of apologies. "Sorry, fella. I'm the fool. No one's fault but my own."

Sophie knelt beside George while Whiskers and Lulu licked his face.

"Ian," Hilary said quietly to the poor man who was once again hiding his face behind his hands, "I think Jean may need you. I see her out on the porch."

Ian shook his head. "Later."

With a shrug, Hilary went outside and came back in with Kim, telling her, "Well, my young friend, I guess you own a painting of two dogs looking down a hole, presumably by one Sir Edwin Landseer."

"And I would guess," I added, "that Ian or the queen or the king of Siam is out one helluva lot of money."

"Cheer up, Ian," Hilary said. "There'll be a paper trail that money seems to leave, and the authorities will dig it out. They say the laws are more relaxed now about the sacred status of Swiss bank accounts. Don't give up hope."

"By the way, Commander." Sophie had risen and assumed her hands-on-hips, don't-kid-me pose. "Just exactly who is the proud owner of the forgery?"

"I can't reveal the name of my client, I'm sorry. The worst thing is" — Ian tried a brave little smile — "I heard from her just hours ago. She loves the painting."

George was happy. "I paid that fellow my last cent to paint that copy. Guess I'll go buy him a drink. Hey, I'm sorry, though, Commander. Kim and I thought it would be asking for trouble if she exhibited the original Landseer at the dog show. Shaw was too tricky for us. Here he's sold my copy to you and was going to sell the original for himself."

Ian probably wasn't listening to George. He asked me, "You tell me, Tish, what am I to do? Do I tell my client she loves a forgery? Wouldn't it make her look less than bright to be taken in that way?"

"Tell her the whole story. She'll love it. She can dine out on it for the next decade."

"But the painting. She'll want the real one."

"That's easy," Kim said. She picked up the critters, who were propped up on the radiator. "I told Mom she could have the painting. She doesn't want it. Said it reminds her of Dad. Right?" she asked Jean, who was standing in the doorway.

Jean nodded.

"She wants me to give it to you, Commander."

Ian's words of gratitude were almost unintelligible as he assured Kim that she'd get her money, not to worry. He, Ian, would not rest until that day.

I could tell from Hil's expression that he was pleasantly surprised at Kim's gracious performance, as was I. I was also delighted when Kim and her mother and Ian, along with Lily and Whiskers, said their good-byes.

"Now, George," Hilary said, "tell me all about the Harvard Business School."

"It's a long story, sir, but briefly, a year ago when I was skiing with Kim, I broke my leg in three places. The pain pills I used became an addiction. It was a bad time. That's when I met you, Mrs. McWhinny, when I was trying, as you said, to rejoin the land of the living. Kim urged me to come to Vermont for the summer. I want you to know, I really was and am still working on a piece about Silas Griffith. Then my Uncle Pete, who's with United Insurance, saved the day and gave me a summer job. Said he wanted me to snoop around and pick up anything I could about expensive cars being stolen in unlikely places. That gave me an objective and a little survival money."

"What did you do in Albany all that time?" Sophie wanted to know. "Tish says you were tailing Connors's helper."

"Yup. It wasn't easy. We got chummy. I told him I was trying to find work. Took a week before he felt safe enough to let me in on what he did. He told me he took Connors's car from that dog show. Connors was to collect the insurance. He showed me the turnaround shop where he and others brought stolen cars. Then they sent them off with new plates, new I.D. numbers and usually new paint jobs."

"Off to?"

"To one of a couple of places where they turned expensive sedans into even more expensive four-door convertibles. Then they'd sell them for megabucks. It didn't take a Sherlock Holmes to figure out who the boss was. None other than Connors."

"Wow, what a story," Sophie said. "You don't need an MBA; you need a word processor."

"Did Kim think up the MBA story?" Hilary asked.

"Yeah. I'm no good at that kind of thing. It made me feel peculiar telling you that lie, sir."

"George," I said, "I want a minute-by-minute report on your sleuthing. However, not now. Please go back to what happened yesterday as we left the dog show. Why did Jack Connors think he owned the dog painting?"

"He said he made a deal with Shaw. Put up a hundred grand to have first refusal on the picture." George dug his wallet out of his back pocket. "Here" — he took out four twenty-dollar bills — "and many thanks, Tish."

"Why in the world," Hilary said, "did Connors want the painting?"

George shrugged. "Just to be a big deal, in keeping with his image. Or perhaps he wanted to make some money selling it to some culture-hungry Texas billionaires. At least that's my guess."

"Or maybe," I said, "he wanted to be sure Ian didn't get it."

The phone rang, and I excused myself to answer it in the kitchen. It was Detective Apple, who said that he had just learned that Shaw had done some talking in custody. Once again I was pleased and surprised at Detective Apple's thoughtfulness. Had I made a new friend? Hanging up, I repeated to everyone in the living room what he'd told me:

Bruce Hemphill owed Shaw money — quite a lot of money. Shaw had given him a couple of paintings to sell, which he had done but failed to pay Shaw. So when he saw the Landseer, he knew he had to get his hands on it one way or another.

Shaw said he saw Jean Connors with Jack walking away from the small clearing near Bruce's motor home, then came upon Bruce holding the awl in one hand and brushing himself off with the other. Shaw hadn't seen the painting anywhere. Disgusted at the drunken Bruce, he shook him and threatened him, and next thing he knew, Bruce had lost his balance and had fallen on the awl. Shaw ran away but he was still determined to get the painting, which he felt belonged to him. When he found out Kim had it, he worked out a scheme to pocket the money and get the painting out of the country. Clearly, George's copy of the painting had made his job easier. Shaw said he planned to sell it to a group who made a business of holding stolen art until the market seemed receptive.

"So he is the murderer." Hilary stood up and stretched. "As you would say, Tish: *pau, fini, kaput*. The end of a very sad story."

"I wonder, Mr. Oats," George said. "Maybe Shaw can talk a jury into thinking

Kim's father died by accident. But since he's confessed to the other stuff — you know, taking Connors's money, and the commander is out Lord knows how much — I expect that kind of larceny would influence a jury. In any event, the man's out of business."

"Out of business? That murderer is out of the civilized world. I'm confident that any jury will see through his lame excuses."

To which I murmured, "Amen." Then, louder: "What do you suppose will happen to Jack Connors? Don't tell me; I know. After hiring expensive lawyers and spending three months in court at our expense, he'll be sent to one of those prisons that doesn't interfere with one's golf game."

"Tell me, Tish," Hilary said, "what do you intend to do with your copy of the painting?"

"Your copy?" George exploded. "You really mean that Tune made another copy? For you?"

I sat there nodding my head. "Yes, indeed he did. Don't think I wasn't surprised to learn about yours. I spoke to him about it yesterday at the dog show. He's totally unrepentant. In fact, he's very pleased with himself. And as to what I'm going to do with my forgery, I share the others' distaste for owning it. I'm going to give it to Lulu's doctor. I think it would look just right on the wall of her waiting room."

George took Sophie's arm. "We had better go, Sophie. You said earlier that Marion is about to have her first kid, and that I want to see."

"Lord, yes. I've been neglecting the goats," Sophie said, getting up. She smiled at me and Hil. "You two ever thought of going someplace serene, as tourists perhaps so you could stay out of trouble? Be on-lookers for a change?"

I looked up at Hilary. "You know, I've been thinking the same thing, dear," I said, "and what I want to do is go to London and spend a week having breakfast in bed every morning and go to the theater every night. All this sinful idleness will take place at the Savoy because my mother as a girl was there for the hotel's gala opening in 1911. Maybe I can con them into giving us a royal suite."

"Great idea." Hilary beamed. "Then let's head north for the second week. I want to see if they really have Scotties in Scotland."

The employees of Thorndike Press hope you have enjoyed this Large Print book. All our Large Print titles are designed for easy reading, and all our books are made to last. Other Thorndike Press Large Print books are available at your library, through selected bookstores, or directly from us.

For information about titles, please call:

(800) 257-5157

To share your comments, please write:

Publisher
Thorndike Press
P.O. Box 159
Thorndike, Maine 04986